# WE ARE THE GIRLS OF BUNK 5A!

### And these are o~~~~~~~

KU-279-140

## Belle
(Counsellor)
My trusty clipboard!

## Clarissa
(CIT – counsellor-in-training)
Spooky stories and ice cream

## Natalie
Fashion mags and
nail polish

## Jenna
Playing pranks!

## Grace
Making new friends!

## Alyssa
Writing in my
journal

## Tori
Shopping, of course!

## Brynn
Broadway shows,
dahling!

## Alex
Sports –
especially soccer

## Gaby
Getting my own way
– kidding!

## Valerie
Dancing my socks off

## Priya
Making up
gross dares

## Chelsea
My cute capri pants

## Candace
My good-luck
worry doll

# SUMMER CAMP SECRETS

Fancy some more sizzling Summer Camp fun?
Check out

**www.summercampsecrets.co.uk**

# Reality Bites

## Melissa.J.Morgan

USBORNE

L192,846/YA

First published in the UK in 2009 by Usborne Publishing Ltd., Usborne House, 83-85 Saffron Hill, London EC1N 8RT, England. www.usborne.com

Copyright © Grosset & Dunlap.
Published by arrangement with Penguin Young Readers Group, a division of Penguin Group (USA) Inc. of 345 Hudson Street, New York, NY 10014, USA. All rights reserved.

Cover photography © Imagestate/Design Pics

The name Usborne and the devices ♀ ⏀ are Trade Marks of Usborne Publishing Ltd.

No part of this publication may be reproduced, stored in a retrieval system or transmitted in any form or by any means, electronic, mechanical, photocopying, recording or otherwise without the prior permission of the publisher.

This is a work of fiction. The characters, incidents, and dialogues are products of the author's imagination and are not to be construed as real. Any resemblance to actual events or persons, living or dead, is entirely coincidental.

A CIP catalogue record for this book is available from the British Library.

ISBN 9781409505549   JFM  MJJASOND /09 89872   Printed in Great Britain.

# CHAPTER ONE

"This is exactly what I needed," Chelsea said suddenly as she and the rest of bunk 5A floated lazily on inflatable rings during free swim. Gaby glanced over at her warily, not sure she wanted to hear the rest. "Peace, quiet and some nice hot rays to soak up. I mean, after everything I went through on our camping trip." Chelsea glanced up to make sure her bunkmates were listening, and Gaby could see that she was trying to look upset. "With Cropsy, and being chased...I was *so* scared, guys."

"We know," Val replied.

"I mean...waking up in an abandoned amusement park? Getting chased by some stranger?"

Tori nodded. "It must have been tough."

"It was, like, horror movie material." Chelsea shuddered.

Gaby looked away. She was annoyed. For almost a week now, Chelsea had been regaling them with tales of her horrible nightmares and flashbacks – all results of a scary time Chelsea had had on their campout, when she got lost and ended up in an abandoned amusement park tended by someone who was rumoured to be a maniac. And Gaby knew it had to have been pretty scary for Chelsea. But she'd come out of it *fine* – the guy, Cropsy, had turned out to be harmless, and Chelsea was safely returned to her bunkmates. *Is she ever going to get over it?* she wondered. For the past two years at camp, Gaby and Chelsea had gotten along okay – they had their share of arguments, but underneath it all they had an understanding. This year, though, they'd had a huge fight at the beginning of camp – and they still hadn't gotten over it. Gaby and Chelsea had barely spoken since the first day.

But now Gaby's bunkmates were making little sympathetic pouts and noises. "It must have been really hard," Brynn cooed. "I mean, we all know Cropsy turned out to be harmless. But still, getting lost in the woods by yourself...and then getting chased..."

"It's really scary," Priya agreed.

Chelsea stopped shuddering, and Gaby watched her try to hide a secret little smile as she tossed her head and leaned back against her ring. "Thanks, guys. I just, you know – it's still hard for me."

Gaby groaned inwardly. To make matters worse, she

*knew* that Chelsea was lying about all the nightmares and flashbacks. She'd seen Chelsea sleeping soundly one night when she claimed she hadn't gotten a wink of sleep because her flashbacks were so bad. And just like now, she'd catch a satisfied expression cross Chelsea's face each time she was supposedly freaking out about this or that – because she'd gotten what she wanted from her bunkmates. Attention.

Gaby wasn't normally one to hold her tongue, and at any other time she would have let Chelsea know exactly what she was thinking. But things were different at Camp Lakeview this year. Not many girls had come back, and Dr. Steve seemed to think it was because Gaby and her friends were "cliquey" and fought too much. That, combined with the totally freaky time they'd had on their overnight (which had gotten weird in just about every way possible, not just where Chelsea was concerned), had led bunk 5A to decide it was time to get along no matter what. Gaby couldn't say anything to Chelsea – she would just end up getting branded as "The Mean Girl".

"Hey," Gaby said, hoping to channel her annoyance into something useful. "Now that we're all rested up, you know what would be fun?"

Priya, who'd been lying back in her rubber ring, half asleep, opened one eye. "What, Gaby?"

7

Gaby smiled encouragingly. "A relay race. Right?"

Slowly, the rest of her bunkmates roused from their relaxation. Gaby could tell from their grumbling that they weren't entirely sold.

"A *race*?" asked Chelsea. "I dunno."

"I'm not in my *athletic* mode," Nat announced in a sleepy voice. "I'm in my *meditation* mode. Changing modes is really difficult."

"Come *on*," Gaby coaxed. She turned to the athletes in the group, the ones she knew would love her idea. "Jenna and Alex, don't you think a race would be fun? We should get some exercise while we're out here. We can't just turn into, like, lake potatoes."

Alex started to smile. "Good point," she said. "A race *totally* sounds fun. I'll be a team captain!"

"Me too," added Jenna.

Gaby pushed off her ring and stood up in the waist-high water. "Guys, it was my idea, so I think *I* should be a team captain," she said cheerfully. This was a great idea — she'd get to lead her team to victory, and everyone would be psyched up. Gaby knew that some of the girls thought she could be bossy or harsh, but she also knew she was a great leader — and the more she could let her friends see that side of her, the better. "And the other captain should be..." Gaby turned to face her bunkmates and grinned. Half of them — the

8

ones who didn't want to have the race in the first place — looked bored. But the *other* half were smiling, nodding, trying to catch Gaby's eye so she would pick them. Gaby decided to be nice. "Chelsea."

Chelsea grinned, looking surprised and pleased, and got off her ring. Pretty soon everyone was doing the same, and they all swam back to the dock to dump their rings there.

"All right, let's choose our teams. Alex," Gaby called.

"Jenna," Chelsea replied.

"Val."

"Priya."

Pretty soon the bunk was split between the two teams, and even the girls who hadn't really wanted to race seemed to be getting into it. Gaby chose the course of the race.

"Each person swims from here to the raft and back, then tags the next person," she announced. "No skipping turns. You have to hit the raft. And once we start, we don't stop *for any reason*." She tried to look each bunkmate in the eye as she surveyed the crowd. "Got it?"

"Got it," agreed Jenna shortly. "Can we start now?"

"Yeah." Brynn, who'd ended up on Chelsea's team with Jenna, smiled. "You're going down! We're gonna crush you!"

"Yeah, *right!*" Alex cried. "You didn't even wanna get off your rubber ring. The *real* athletes are all on this team!"

"What?!" Jenna cried.

"You know what I mean." Alex looked away and tried to shrug.

"Whatever," Chelsea piped up. "At least we're not all busy *meditating*—"

Gaby rushed to interrupt before a fully fledged fight broke out. "Channel that energy into your swimming, ladies! All right. Alex and Jenna swim first. On your mark...get set...*go!*"

"Come on, Jenna!"

"Go get 'em, Alex!"

Priya and Val got into position as Alex and Jenna each slapped the raft and headed back – Alex with a very slight lead over Jenna.

"Come on, come on, come on!" Gaby shouted to Alex. "Keep it moving! We've got to beat Ch – the other team!"

Val took off, followed closely by Priya. Gaby smiled, watching Val gain a small lead. Everything was going perfectly. She'd put herself in the all-important last slot, so that when her team won, *she* would be the one to actually win it for them. Her teammates would be thrilled. Glancing over at Chelsea, she noticed a frown pulling at the corners of her mouth.

Chelsea glanced up just in time to see Gaby watching her. "What are you looking at?" she demanded.

Gaby bristled. She pasted on a fake smile. "Oh, Chelsea," she said, "let's not pick fights with each other. We need peace and quiet, remember?"

Chelsea didn't say anything, but her glare was strong enough to burn holes through Gaby's shirt.

Natalie and Tori were swimming back to the dock now. Natalie swam up to the dock, panting, and tagged Gaby's ankle. Taking a deep breath, Gaby jumped into the lake. She felt the cool water gush over her head, then pushed back up to the surface and started swimming towards the raft.

Gaby wasn't actually that strong a swimmer, but her team already had a nice lead over Chelsea's team. She was halfway to the raft when she heard the *splash* of Chelsea jumping into the lake.

In a few seconds Gaby was at the raft and reached out her hand to slap it. Then she pushed off the raft and started swimming back. She looked back at the dock, expecting to see Chelsea dog-paddling not too far from where she'd just jumped in. But Chelsea was nowhere to be seen. Gaby paused for a second as a horrible thought crossed her mind. *Did she sink or something?* She knew Chelsea wasn't the strongest swimmer, but she'd never thought...

*WHACK! SPLASH!* Gaby heard someone smacking the raft right behind her, and was suddenly totally soaked by a wave of water. Right before her head went under, she saw a blur of red swim by — *Chelsea's red bathing suit!* Chelsea was now a couple of metres ahead of her, swimming with a fierce determination. *Since when does Chelsea swim like that?* Gaby wondered, diving forward to try to catch up. She paddled wildly, really using all of the energy she had this time. *Since you made her mad,* she realized, kicking like crazy. *You provoked Chelsea, and now she's mad enough to want to win. Way to go.*

Gaby tried to ignore everything that was going on around her and just concentrate on catching up to Chelsea's red bathing suit. Soon her lungs were burning, and so were the muscles in her arms and legs.

"Go, Gaby! Come on, come on, come on!"

"You can still win this!"

But no matter what Gaby did, Chelsea remained out in front. Gaby realized that Chelsea was actually a pretty good swimmer when she tried. She just usually didn't. *Smack!* With one fluid motion, Chelsea brought her arm up and tagged the dock, winning the race for her team, who all erupted in cheers. "Way to go, Chelsea!" Jenna yelled. "I guess we showed them who the *real* athletes are."

"Hey, c'mon," called Alex, frowning at her friend.

"That's not what I said. I just meant – you know."

"Whatever," Jenna shrugged and looked away. "We won. That's what matters."

Gaby finally reached the dock, panting and totally spent. Her lungs were on fire, and her throat still burned from breathing in water when she'd been submerged by the Chelsea wave. She grabbed the dock and just hung on, looking down into the water, trying to catch her breath.

"Tough luck, Gaby," Chelsea said with a little smile, climbing out of the water and onto the dock. "Maybe try a little harder next time."

Gaby coughed and pushed her wet hair back off her face. *Since when are you an athlete?* she thought, but she bit the words back. She took a few deep breaths.

"It's cool, Gaby," Natalie spoke up, twisting a lock of hair around her finger. "You tried hard."

"Yeah, totally," Candace agreed, reaching down a hand to help Gaby climb onto the dock. "You know, we had fun, that's what matters."

Gaby took Candace's hand and pulled herself up onto the dock, still panting.

"You know, everyone has a talent," Chelsea said with a sickly sweet smile. "I guess yours is...something other than swimming."

Gaby was on her feet now, reaching for her towel.

She was still trying to take deep breaths and blow off Chelsea's poorly concealed insult. But she felt her face reddening.

"You know what? Can it!" she cried, wagging her towel in Chelsea's direction. "I don't need any encouragement from you."

"Come on, Gaby," Natalie said, reaching out to touch her shoulder. "Be nice. They won fair and square."

*Fair and square.* Gaby knew it was true, but she still couldn't believe it. There had to be *some* way she could have won. She could still imagine herself reaching the dock first, and her whole team erupting in cheers. Instead she had barked at Chelsea, and now everyone thought she was mean again. There had to be a reason her perfect plan had failed. "Natalie! *You* lost half our lead over Chelsea's team!" she cried, not pausing to think it through. It was true, Nat had lost a little bit of their lead because she wasn't a great swimmer. But it hadn't really been enough to make a difference. "If you were a better swimmer, we would have won."

Natalie's face went from concerned to stunned. "Are you *kidding*?" she asked. "Look, *you're* the one who wanted to have this stupid race in the first place. I did my best."

"Natalie swam fine," Alex agreed, and a bunch of the other girls grunted their agreement. "We *all* did fine. It was a fair race, and we lost." She walked over to Gaby and stood right in front of her, looking down. Her eyes weren't angry – that's what killed Gaby. They were concerned, like her parents' had been when she'd gotten busted for cheating on a test back home. It was like she'd said something so crazy it wasn't even worth arguing about, and Alex was more worried about her. "You need to chill out, Gaby. It was just for fun, anyway. Grow up."

Gaby felt like she'd been slapped. She felt tears burning her eyes, but she looked down and picked at her towel so the other girls wouldn't see them. "Whatever," she muttered.

In the awkward silence that followed, one of the counsellors blew the whistle that meant free swim was over. All the girls grabbed their towels and flip-flops and started wrapping themselves up, strolling off towards the cabin.

"The funniest thing happened during the nature walk this morning," Brynn suddenly piped up.

"What?" Tori asked eagerly, like she was happy to put Gaby's weird behaviour behind them.

"Well, we came upon this clearing, right? And there's all this..."

Gaby tuned out and blinked a few times, clearing her eyes. She grabbed her towel and stood up, slowly wrapping it around herself. Her bunkmates strolled casually ahead of her, in twos and threes, all now involved in separate conversations. Gaby trailed along behind them, not really part of any group.

*Nobody gives me any attention*, she thought, *unless it's the wrong kind*. She sighed. Gaby knew she had a harsh edge – but her friends at home also thought she was funny, and they knew that when she liked you, she was totally loyal. At camp, nobody seemed to understand Gaby. She'd say something snarky and funny, but her bunkmates would only pick up on the *snarky* part. She knew she was being kind of a jerk about the race – but only because she had really hoped to win, and then Chelsea had gone and said something dumb. She couldn't resist responding – could she?

Dragging her feet along the trail, Gaby stubbed her toe on a root. "Ow!" she cried, without thinking about it.

"You okay?" Alyssa asked, turning from her conversation with Jenna.

"I stubbed my toe," Gaby said quietly.

Jenna raised her eyebrows. "Is it okay? Does it still hurt?"

Gaby looked down at her toe. Honestly, it felt fine now – just one more toe among the millions that had probably been stubbed on that root. But the way Jenna and Alyssa were looking at her, all concerned and friendly – she wanted them to look at her that way more often.

"It really does," she replied, reaching down to touch it. "I hope I didn't break it!"

Priya, Val and Tori paused in their conversation now. "What's up?" Priya asked.

"Gaby stubbed her toe kind of hard," Jenna explained. "She thinks it might be broken."

Pretty soon all of the bunkmates were circled around Gaby, all looking sympathetic and concerned.

"It's kind of numb," Gaby lied. "I think I'd better go to the infirmary."

"I'll go with you," Alex offered. "We should go right away, right after we change!"

Brynn offered to let Gaby lean on her to hobble back to the cabin, and Gaby gratefully accepted. Together, they all walked the five hundred metres or so back to their bunk. Soon the conversation shifted away from Gaby's toe, but this time, they were all together and Gaby was part of it. The icky feeling she'd had on the dock was forgotten.

Their counsellor, Belle, was sitting outside the cabin on a big rock, waiting for them to come back. "Hey, guys!" she cried, jumping up as soon as they came out of the woods. "Have I got a surprise for you! You're going to be *so* psyched!"

"What's up?" asked Natalie, walking ahead to the cabin.

Belle pulled open the cabin door, and out walked Grace. All the girls went wild.

"*Grace!*" cried Alex. "I thought summer school didn't end till next week? I missed you so much!"

Pretty soon everyone was gathered around Grace, shooting questions at her, talking about how much they'd missed her, how camp hadn't seemed the same without her. Gaby hung back on the outside of the crowd, trying to conceal her annoyance. Grace was *fine*. There was nothing wrong with Grace. Gaby was the one who was hurt.

It was half an hour — after all the girls had changed and had been hanging around talking for another ten minutes — before anyone remembered Gaby's broken toe.

"Hey," Brynn said suddenly, jumping up from her bunk. "Don't you have to go to the infirmary, Gaby? I thought your toe was, like, about to fall off."

Gaby sighed. She was sitting alone on a bunk across the room, while everyone else was crowded onto two bunks, questioning Grace. "You know what?" she said. "It actually feels fine now. Forget it."

L192,846/YA

# CHAPTER TWO

"It feels *amazing* to be back," Grace was telling her best friend, Brynn, as they walked to the mess hall for lunch. "Omigosh, summer school was *so* boring. Two weeks of sitting in a classroom, when all I could think about was being out here with you guys!"

Brynn smiled. "It's good to have you back, Grace," she said. "I missed you like crazy! It felt like we were missing something without you. Maybe that's why things got so weird while you were gone."

"What do you mean?" Grace asked. But before Brynn could answer, Chelsea ran up to them.

"So," she interrupted, "notice anything *different* about camp this year, Grace?"

Grace shrugged. "I've only been here half an hour."

Chelsea nodded and gestured to the other kids gathered around the mess hall. "I'll give you a hint," she said. "It's not about who you see. It's about who you *don't* see."

Grace scanned the crowd outside the mess hall. She felt the corners of her mouth drooping as she noticed how few people she recognized. She knew Sarah and Abby had gone to sports camp. But there was no Karen. No Jessie. No Tiernan. Of course she'd noticed they weren't in bunk 5A, but she'd assumed they'd still come to camp and were just in another bunk. Now she realized they actually hadn't come.

"Why?" Grace asked, unable to keep the disappointment out of her voice. "I mean, so many people are missing. Cool people. Did something happen?"

Chelsea snorted. "A lot happened in the two weeks you weren't here, Grace. But I don't know why so many people didn't come to camp. They just decided not to come." She leaned in and whispered into Grace's ear: "Dr. Steve thinks it's because we're too *cliquey.*"

Grace frowned. "Us? Cliquey? Do you really think that's why they didn't come back?" Grace had always been tight with her camp friends, but it had never occurred to her that other girls might feel left out.

Chelsea shrugged. "I don't know. You'd have to ask the girls that didn't come. Look, the doors are opening. I'm starved."

As Chelsea ran off into the mess hall, Grace looked at Brynn. "It must be weird with half the group gone."

Brynn sighed. "It was *really* weird for a while, but things seem to have calmed down now. I'm just glad *you're* here. Let's eat."

Inside the mess hall, most of the bunk had already sat down at their usual table. Brynn had to show Grace where it was, over in the corner near the fireplace. Conversation was already going strong when Grace and Brynn joined them.

"It's the *best* female part," Nat was explaining to Alex. "Adelaide is, like, the centre of the whole show. She has the best song. My dad took me to see it on Broadway a couple of years ago."

"Wow," Alex said. "Congrats, Brynn! Nat was just telling us about your new role."

"What are you talking about?" Grace asked as their CIT, Clarissa, reached the table with a tray of sloppy joes.

"The play this session," Brynn replied, reaching for a sandwich. "It's *Guys and Dolls*, and I'm playing Adelaide."

Grace felt her heart sink. She knew the music for *Guys and Dolls* by heart — her mom was a huge fan of musicals and played the cast album when she was doing housework. "Wow. Good for you, Brynn. Um, I guess you guys already chose electives, then?"

Tori nodded, looking at her like she was nuts. "Oh, *yeah*," she said. "Last Friday, so..." She paused to grab a sandwich, looking concerned. "I wonder what they'll have you do? Since we have electives after lunch. You won't have anywhere to go!"

Belle, who was sitting a seat away on Grace's right, reached over and squeezed her shoulder. "No worries, Grace," she promised. "We'll get you some electives. You might have to wait till next session to get your first choices, though." She pushed back her chair and stood up. "Actually, I'll go now and see what electives have space for you."

Chelsea smirked. "Yeah, hope you like nature." Nature was always the last elective to fill up. Grace actually didn't mind it — sometimes it required touching slime or getting a little dirty to collect "specimens", but that was cool with her.

"Actually, a few of us are in the show," Brynn said, gesturing at Gaby. "Gaby is playing Sarah Brown, Candace is in the chorus, and David's playing Nathan Detroit."

Jenna smiled. She and David were in like-like territory. "He'll make a good gangster, too, if he can stop goofing off for five minutes."

Grace glanced at Gaby. Sarah Brown was her favourite role in the show — it wasn't the biggest part,

22

but she had Grace's favourite song, "If I Were a Bell".

"That's great," Grace said encouragingly. "I mean, good for you, Gaby. That's a really great role."

Gaby was busy picking the onions out of her sloppy joe. She looked up, surprised at Grace's compliment, but still wore a bored expression. "Thanks, I guess." She shrugged. "It's not as cool as Adelaide."

"You just got interested in drama, like, *yesterday*," said Brynn. She sounded like she was trying hard *not* to sound annoyed. "You're not going to waltz right in and play the best part. I've been acting since I was eight."

Gaby glanced over at Brynn, still looking bored, and shrugged. "I guess..."

Brynn looked like she was about to boil over, but Nat cut her at the pass, talking ten to the dozen. "You have more than one song, Gaby. It's a really important role, and I'm sure the play will be great." She took a deep breath and turned to Grace. "Change of subject! How was summer school?"

Grace shrugged. "You know. It was boring. All I could think about was finishing up and getting up here."

Chelsea nodded. "You missed *so* much, t – *ow!*"

Alex was elbowing her in the side. "She *knows* that, Chelsea. It's not a big deal." She looked over at Grace and lowered her voice confidentially, even though she was all the way across the table. "Seriously, Grace?

Most of the stuff you missed, you should be glad."

"Well, Nat filled me in on the camping trip and that Cropsy story," Grace said defensively. "So I kind of know all about—"

Chelsea cut Grace off. "Guys? Seriously. Let's not even bring him up. I'd like to sleep tonight."

Suddenly everyone looked sympathetic. Except for Gaby, who was murdering her sloppy joe crust with a fork. And Grace, who was lost in thought. Why did she feel like she was fighting for her right to belong?

"Sorry, Chelsea," Alex said with an apologetic smile. "I forgot you still get scared."

Every girl seemed to go into her own world, nodding or shaking her head. Grace took a few bites of her sloppy joe, waiting for an explanation, but her friends seemed to have forgotten she was there.

"That's not even all," Jenna piped up after a few minutes. "Remember Dr. Steve's lecture? The reason we had to go on the overnight in the first place?"

Everyone moaned. "It's so stupid," said Chelsea. "We're not cliquey. We're nice to everyone!"

Grace put down her sandwich and looked around the table. She felt so out of the loop. "Um. Guys?"

"Totally!" Priya was saying. "Anyone could just sit down at our table and feel completely at home. We're equal opportunity."

"Guys?" Grace asked again.

"All right, Grace!" Grace felt a hand on the back of her shoulder and turned to face Belle, who was smiling and holding a piece of notepaper. "I apologize in advance – you're going to have to go where we have room for you this session. That means if you had your heart set on sports or drama, you might be disappointed." Belle handed Grace the piece of paper. She had scrawled CERAMICS AND NEWSPAPER in her funky handwriting. "You'll have newspaper this afternoon. And then you can start ceramics tomorrow morning."

Grace felt a little disappointed. She knew that auditions had already passed, but she'd hoped – a little ridiculously, she realized now – that maybe she could be squeezed into drama and just put in the chorus or something. Now she realized that wasn't going to happen. And it stunk, because she only wanted to be in the play because it was *Guys and Dolls*, and when was Camp Lakeview ever going to mount that show again? Never.

Still, she tried to smile. Ceramics was okay, and while she'd never worked on the newspaper before, she was sure she'd learn something about...something. It would be very "educational", as her mother would say.

Or something.

Just as Grace was about to thank Belle and ask about

the camping/cliquey stuff again, the bell rang signalling the end of lunch. Before Grace could open her mouth, everyone was on their feet, forming little twos and threes and heading off in different directions. Grace looked down at the paper and sighed, shoving it in her pocket. When she looked up, Alyssa and Candace were standing there, waiting.

"Come on, Grace!" Alyssa said with a big smile. "Look at you, two weeks of school and you're already all slow and out of it."

Grace laughed in spite of herself. "I'll get back into the camp groove. Just give me a couple days."

"Come on," said Alyssa, gesturing towards the door. "Candace and I are in newspaper, too. I think you're really going to like it."

"Totally," agreed Candace. "You'll totally like it."

They turned and started walking as Grace pushed back her chair and stood. "I hope so," she muttered under her breath.

"Seriously?" Dana, the counsellor who taught newspaper, scrunched up her blonde eyebrows in surprise. Her hair was twisted and stuck to her head with pencils jutting out in various directions, and she looked a little frazzled. "They told you to come here?"

Grace nodded. "My counsellor, Belle, did," she explained. "She said you guys have room? I mean, if you *don't*, that's cool, maybe I can squeeze into drama..."

Dana frowned and shook her head. "No, forget that. They've already cast and started rehearsals. You'll be fine here, it's just..." She paused to look around the room. "We'll need to find something for you to do."

"Maybe I can help Alyssa and Candace?" Grace suggested. Her bunkmates were already camped out in front of a computer, researching on the internet for some big article they were working on.

"Nah." Dana shook her head. "They're halfway done with a big opinion piece about donating the camp's leftover food to a shelter. I don't like to put more than two people on one article – it gets distracting."

Grace nodded. Alyssa and Candace did seem to be totally in the zone. In fact, within two minutes of reaching the newspaper room, Grace felt like they'd forgotten she was ever there.

"I know!" Dana smiled as her eyes settled on a table across the room. "I'll put you on the arts column with Spence. He could probably use a little help."

Grace followed her gaze and saw Spence, a guy who had been crushing on Priya last summer, sitting at a table surrounded by scraps of notepaper. Dana leaned in and whispered, "He's a little disorganized." Grace couldn't help smiling. She hadn't talked much to Spence the summer before, but he seemed like a nice guy. And maybe if she made herself useful, she could shake this weird *unnecessary* feeling.

"Hey!" she called, walking over to Spence. "Spence! I think I'm going to be helping you out."

Spence glanced up, examining Grace with light blue eyes that sparkled through his glasses. His hair stuck up a little bit where he'd been leaning his head on his hand. "I know you," he said slowly. "You're Priya's friend. And Chelsea's. Right?"

Grace nodded. "I'm Grace," she said. "I was at summer school the first two weeks of camp, and I missed electives sign-up, so they kind of stuck me in here." She stopped short, wondering if that sounded snotty. She didn't want to make it sound like she didn't want to be there, or like she was too good for newspaper or something. "I mean, they put me in here, and I'm totally psyched to work on the arts column with you—"

"Great," Spence said agreeably, standing up and grabbing his notebook and a recorder off the table. "'Cause I think we'd better get started on our first assignment. The play!"

"The play?" Grace asked, her excitement faltering.

"The play." Spence shuffled around the scraps of paper until he found the one he wanted. "They're doing *Guys and Girls*?"

"*Guys and Dolls*," Grace corrected him. "It's a musical. About gangsters."

Spence tucked his scrap paper into his pocket and grinned at Grace. "See?" he said, placing his hand on Grace's back and guiding her to the door. "You were born for the arts beat."

"Didn't you used to hang out with Devon last summer?" Spence asked as they walked over to the gym, where rehearsals were being held.

Grace smiled. "Yeah, a little," she agreed as they walked up the gym steps. "I haven't seen him yet! I can't wait to catch up."

"Well, that's going to be hard to do," Spence said, grabbing the door. "Unless you have a plane. Devon's in Hawaii this summer with his parents."

Grace felt her heart sink a little deeper in her chest. It wasn't like she and Devon had been serious or anything — they'd exchanged a few e-mails over the past year — but she'd liked the idea of having someone else who'd be happy to see her.

"Bummer," she muttered.

"Not for Devon!" Spence said cheerfully. "Seriously, how much would you love being on a tropical beach right now, drinking out of a coconut? I'm so jealous of that guy." He glanced at Grace and flashed a quick smile. "I mean, Camp Lakeview's almost as nice."

"Right." Grace chuckled. Up onstage, Brynn was rehearsing her big number, "Adelaide's Lament". Grace had to stop herself from mouthing the words along with the song. In a corner, she spotted Gaby reading a magazine and totally not paying attention. Gaby tended to zone out sometimes — especially when she felt people weren't paying enough attention to *her*.

Grace sighed.

"What's up?" Spence asked, shooting her a concerned look. "You and Devon weren't that serious, were you?"

Grace shook her head. "No, not at all. I mean, I liked him. It's just..."

Spence tilted his head sympathetically. "Now you don't know how to tell him you're dumping him for me?"

Grace couldn't help it. She busted out laughing. "HA! Ha ha ha! Oh, please..."

Spence was laughing, too, but he seemed more in control of himself. He clamped a hand over Grace's mouth to stop her from disrupting the rehearsals. It was too late, though. The music had stopped, and Brynn was squinting to see who was losing their composure over at the far side of the gym.

"Grace?" Brynn asked. "Is that you?"

Grace tried to take deep breaths, calming herself down. It was tough, though. Somehow the horribleness of stopping the whole rehearsal made the whole thing seem even *funnier* and more ridiculous. "It's — hee-hee — it's me, Brynn. Sorry. I just — remembered something really funny."

Brynn smiled a little, like she was trying to understand. "What are you doing here?"

"We're covering the play for the newspaper!" Spence called. "We just...had a moment back here. Sorry to interrupt."

Brynn glanced quizzically at Grace again, then back at the piano player. The music started again and Brynn went back to singing. The last thing Grace noticed before turning back to Spence was Gaby, her attention now totally on Grace and Spence, scowling in their direction.

"You *jerk!*" Grace whispered, but she was still smiling. "No. For your *information*, I was just sighing because of this play. I wanted to be in it."

"Really?" Spence pulled out his notebook and made a couple of notes. "You like acting?"

Grace shrugged. "Sometimes. I've done it before. But I really like this play."

"How do you know it?" Spence asked, still scribbling. It was weird – Grace knew he wasn't scribbling about her, but she still felt like he was paying total attention to their conversation. It impressed her that he could do two things at once.

"My mom," Grace replied. "She likes musicals. She plays the cast album all the time."

Spence stopped writing and stuck his pen in his jeans pocket. "That's cool," he said. "My uncle's way into plays. He takes me whenever something good comes to DC. I just saw *Wicked*."

Grace was surprised. Most of the guys she knew would rather die than admit they'd seen some girly musical. But Spence seemed totally unbothered. "What part would you want to play?" he asked her.

"Sarah Brown," Grace replied without thinking.

Spence looked surprised. "That's not the lead, is it?"

Grace shook her head. "The lead is Nathan, or for a girl, Adelaide. I just like Sarah's song."

"No kidding?" Spence asked. He really seemed interested, Grace realized. "You a good singer?"

Grace shrugged. "I'm no Leona Lewis, but I do all right."

Spence laughed. He looked back at the stage, where the whole cast was now gathered to rehearse a group number. "Well, it looks like we're going to have to wait to get our interviews. Why don't you sing a little for me?"

Grace blushed. "You *must* be kidding."

Spence just smiled and shook his head. "Come on. Show me a little of that Sarah Brown spirit."

"Um, won't it disrupt the rehearsal?" Grace looked up at the stage. Everyone seemed to have forgotten she and Spence were there. "They're singing, you know."

"All the better." Spence raised his eyebrows, grinning. "They won't even hear you. Only I will."

Grace sighed. She totally hadn't been planning to show off when she'd told Spence she wanted to be in the play. After all, it was too late anyway – no matter how she sounded, she wasn't going to play Sarah Brown. But fine. If Spence wanted to be entertained by her well-practised version of "If I Were a Bell", then entertained he would be.

Grace took a deep breath and started singing quietly.

Once she started singing, Grace relaxed. The song was so familiar to her, but she still found something new and interesting in the lyrics every time she sang it. Pretty soon she was lost in the music, imagining herself up onstage, singing her heart out. Grace wasn't obsessed

33

with acting, not the way Brynn was, but she had to admit she liked being onstage – and she missed it.

Suddenly Grace was aware of a change in the air. She opened her eyes. *Oh no.* The music had stopped, and the cast wasn't all up onstage any more. Grace turned and almost jumped two metres in the air when she realized that Gaby was standing right next to her. Gaby's expression was strange – she was smiling, but her eyes didn't look happy. They looked...something else. *Scared*, maybe.

"*Wow*," Gaby said, her hands on her hips. "That was great, Grace. I didn't know you knew my song."

"Yeah, well." Grace shrugged and tried to look away. She knew there was no reason to feel guilty – Gaby still had the role no matter what – but she did. "My mom plays the album a lot. 'If I Were a Bell' is my favourite song."

Gaby nodded, never taking her eyes of Grace's face. "Interesting. Well, what a *cute* voice you have. Not a lot of power, but..."

Grace cringed.

"...really *sweet*." Gaby smiled. But Grace was chilled by the smile.

"Thanks," Grace muttered, hoping the conversation would end now.

"I think she has a great voice," Spence piped up

34

suddenly. He turned to Gaby, pushing his glasses up on his nose. "If she sounded quiet, it's because she was trying not to mess up the rehearsals. My bad. I told her I wanted to hear her sing."

Gaby turned to Spence with a death stare. "Sarah Brown is my role. And yeah, it is actually really distracting for you guys to be singing."

Spence held up his hands. "Sorry! Listen, do you want to be interviewed for the newspaper?"

Grace turned to Spence and gave him a huge smile. Perfect! How did he know that the way to calm Gaby down was to give her the attention she was always looking for?

The anger in Gaby's eyes died away all at once and a smile played at the corners of her lips. "You want to interview me? Sure! Should we go someplace quiet?"

She grabbed Spence's arm and led him to a far corner of the gym as the pianist started up again and David got up onstage to start practising. As Gaby was dragging him away, Spence turned around and winked at Grace. He mouthed to her in an exaggerated way: *"You were great."*

Grace felt a warmth spreading over her whole body. *I was great.*

She had a feeling she was going to like newspaper after all.

# CHAPTER THREE

Gaby picked at her hamburger, trying to fish out the onions that she hated but which were in every Camp Lakeview dish. Seriously, what was up with the onions? Did onions really belong in hamburgers? It had to be some kind of conspiracy.

All around her, Gaby's bunkmates were exchanging stories about their day. Across the table, Grace was laughing with Candace and Alyssa, telling a story about something she and Spence had done for newspaper. Gaby sighed. *Why would Grace come into our rehearsal and totally steal my spotlight?* she wondered. Spence had interviewed her for the article they were writing, but then he and Grace had also interviewed Brynn and practically every other member of the cast. Gaby wasn't stupid. She knew she'd get maybe one quote in the newspaper, if she was lucky – and probably about something like how good *Brynn* sounded in her role.

Not anything about *her*, how good she was. Not anything that would make her bunkmates notice her — for a good reason, this time.

Gaby studied Grace, taking a tiny bite of hamburger. *What was that about?* she wondered, thinking back to Grace's impromptu song. *Was she trying to show me up?* Gaby couldn't understand it. Grace already had plenty of friends — she was one of the most popular girls in their bunk. Everyone loved her. Why would she go out of her way to get *more* attention — and take it away from Gaby, who really needed it more?

*It doesn't matter*, Gaby told herself as she felt her face growing hot. *My voice is better than hers. I know it is.* Still, it wasn't cool what Grace had done. As Grace excused herself to use the bathroom, Gaby wondered again why she'd started singing in the first place — what were she and Spence up to, anyway?

"Hey," whispered Priya, as soon as Grace was out of earshot. "Did you guys see who Grace was giggling with on the way to the mess hall?"

Everyone looked up, puzzled. "No," Alex replied neutrally. "Who?"

"*Spence.*" Priya leaned in and bugged her eyes out like she was saying *Madonna*.

Gaby watched Priya, thinking. Priya and Chelsea had both had a crush on Spence when camp started, but after things had gotten so crazy on their camping trip, they decided that neither one would go after him — that getting along was more important. They called Spence "neutral territory". But Gaby was sceptical. She knew that when a girl really crushed on a guy, like Chelsea and Priya had, those feelings didn't just go away overnight. It stood to reason that both of them still liked him. Why were they trying to hide it?

"They're in newspaper together," Gaby explained. "They came to rehearsal to write about the play. And actually..." Gaby remembered how Grace and Spence had erupted in giggles when they first came in. She remembered how close they stood, whispering back and forth about something — who knew what?

"What?" Chelsea asked after a few seconds. "Actually, *what*?"

Gaby shrugged. "They seemed kind of flirty," she said honestly. She tried to think of the phrase the gossip mags her mother read all the time used...*aha!* "In fact, you might say they were...*canoodling*."

Everyone's mouth dropped open. Gaby smiled. It felt good to be the first one with new information.

"*Canoodling?*" Priya gasped.

"Canoodling?" asked Brynn, looking doubtful.

"Canoodling," Gaby returned. "Yeah, it was while

you were onstage, Brynn, not paying attention. I thought it was weird, actually, since they'd never hung out before. But whatever."

Chelsea and Priya both looked dumbfounded. "Wow," Chelsea whispered.

Gaby had to suppress her smile. Somehow, some way, she needed to keep this conversation going. Spence had been the object of a ton of crushes this year – maybe there was something in that? "I can't believe she's going after *Spence* of all people," she said.

"What's *that* supposed to mean?" Natalie asked, putting down her fork.

Gaby cringed. *I did it again. I crossed the line.*

Nat went on, "I don't get what the big deal is. Priya, Chelsea, you don't like him any more, right? He's – what did you call him?"

"Neutral territory," Chelsea whispered.

"Right." Nat nodded, looking from Chelsea to Gaby and back. "Neutral territory. And besides, we all know Spence is a huge flirt. It's not exactly a surprise that he'd flirt with Grace. So what's the big deal if she *does* date him?"

Gaby opened her mouth and tried to come up with an answer, but before she could, Priya spoke up.

"It's not a big deal," Priya said a little too quickly, seeming to shake off her trance. "*Of course* Chelsea and

I don't like him. It's just surprising that Grace would move so fast. Right, Chelse?"

Chelsea sat up in her seat and seemed to come back to life. "Right," she said quietly.

"We're just *happy* for Grace," Priya went on. "I mean, for her to find somebody she likes like that. It's hard for me to imagine liking Spence like that, since I'm *so* over him. But I'm glad Grace found somebody, especially since Devon didn't come back this year." She glanced at Chelsea, who still looked less than happy. "Right?" she asked pointedly. "Aren't we happy, Chelse?"

"Sure," Chelsea replied, still wearing no traces of any expression that might imply happiness. "Happy."

Gaby looked from Priya to Chelsea. It didn't take a brain surgeon to see that they were lying. But why? "Are you *sure*?" she asked insistently. "I mean, it's hard to get over someone so fast. Even if you didn't still *like* him" — she looked at Priya — "it would be weird to see him with someone else so soon."

"It's *fine*," Priya replied, attacking her hamburger with gusto. "Please. Spence is so five minutes ago."

Alyssa smiled. "So who's the new Spence?"

Priya chewed a huge bite of hamburger and swallowed, washing it down with some bug juice. "TBD."

Gaby grinned. To Be Determined. *Yeah, right.*

In the silence that followed, Grace returned from the bathroom and sat down, looking around at her bunkmates' silent faces. "Hey, guys," she said hesitantly. "Wow, if I didn't know better, I'd be worried you guys were talking about me. The way total silence fell when I came back."

Gaby turned to her, remembering the moment Grace's voice had interrupted their rehearsal. What was Grace's deal, anyway? What *was* going on with her and Spence? Gaby decided to just ask. "What's up with you and Spence, Grace?"

Grace looked at Gaby like she was speaking Russian. *The who in the what-now?* "Huh?" she asked softly. "Me and *Spence*? What about us?"

"There have been rumours," Brynn explained, "of the two of you *canoodling*."

Grace let out a laugh. "Canoodling?" she asked. "Where, in the *Camp Lakeview Enquirer*? I think you should check your source on that."

Everyone turned to Gaby.

Gaby wasn't sure what to say. She'd seen Grace and Spence, lost in their own little world on the other side of the gym. Wasn't that what *canoodling* was? She needed a dictionary. "Maybe I didn't see what I thought I saw," Gaby said. "But you guys did seem close. I mean, you were definitely hanging out."

Grace looked confused. "We were working together on an article for the newspaper."

Gaby sighed. "But don't you *like* him," she said.

Grace looked even more confused.

Priya leaned over and patted Grace's hand. "Seriously, Grace, I think it's great if you like him. Don't worry about me. I mean, he's really cute."

"And funny," Chelsea added in a forlorn voice.

"And if you like him," Priya added, spearing a tater tot with excessive force, "maybe you guys can go to the *social* together! You'd have a great time."

There was a loud clatter as Chelsea dropped her fork.

"Um," said Grace, looking at her friends, then at her hands. "He's nice. I guess. I mean—"

"And he *is* cute," Gaby interrupted, pointing her bug juice cup at Grace. "Right?"

Grace looked at Gaby like a deer caught in the headlights. Gaby didn't get it. *Why is she acting like she has no idea what I'm talking about?* "Right," Grace replied softly.

"Those *glasses*," Priya said with a sigh, shaking her head. "I mean, they don't do anything for me, any more. But I can still see the appeal."

"Those eyes," Chelsea added, nodding. "So blue."

Everyone seemed to look at Grace at once. She still looked confused. "I guess," she said finally. She pushed in her chair and took a sip of bug juice. "I guess he's really cute."

"Awww!" cried Gaby.

"So *sweet!*" echoed Candace.

"Ah, young love," Brynn added, but her expression was still sceptical. "Well, good for you, Grace. I'm glad you met someone to crush on so fast."

"Yeah," added Alex.

"Yeah," whispered Chelsea.

"Um, thanks," replied Grace, looking around the table at her bunkmates. She felt like she had never seen these people before in her life. "I guess."


"Have I got a surprise for you!" Dr. Steve was standing in front of the fireplace in the mess hall as everyone finished up dessert and got ready for the campfire.

"What is it?" called out one of the boys from the fourth division. Pretty soon others joined in; shouts of "yeah!" and "what?" turned into a dull roar that filled the mess hall.

Dr. Steve just smiled. "Well," he said finally, and the hall immediately turned silent, "who misses TV?"

The mess hall erupted in total chaos. Gaby blocked her ears as, all around her, campers whooped, hollered and high-fived one another. "Stupid," she muttered under her breath. "You don't even know what it is yet."

Dr. Steve gestured for the campers to calm down, and soon the hall was quiet again. "I have a friend who works in television," he explained, "who told me about a new TV show that's running this summer. It's called *Survival Camp*, and it's a reality game show, like *Survivor*."

At the mention of their favourite show, many campers started shouting. Dr. Steve made the "quiet" gesture again, then continued.

"The difference is, it's about a group of kids your age. They camp for two weeks under very harsh conditions, and at the end, one kid is the winner. That kid, along with his or her whole family, will win an all-expenses-paid trip to Australia. But most importantly, *all* of the kids on the show will learn an important lesson about teamwork."

Gaby cringed. "Teamwork" was a word she'd heard a lot of lately – in Dr. Steve's lectures to their bunk about their "cliqueyness". She had a feeling she knew where this was going.

"Teamwork is something that's very important to me," Dr. Steve went on. "I hope that you'll leave Camp Lakeview with some tangible skills – how to canoe, how to camp safely, how to identify constellations, and much more." He paused. "But more importantly, I hope

44

you'll leave Camp Lakeview with some character skills. Things like teamwork, respect and cooperation. Those skills will be even more helpful to you throughout your life."

Gaby sighed. The truth was, she was sick of hearing about Dr. Steve's "character skills" – and more than that, she was sick of being told that she, and all the rest of the girls in her bunk, didn't have any.

"It's become clear to me that many of our campers could benefit from a little lesson on teamwork," Dr. Steve continued, glancing at Gaby's table. Gaby looked away. "So I've decided that maybe you kids could use a little TV time."

The noise level in the mess hall ratcheted up from about three to about three *thousand*. Gaby cringed as all the campers whooped, yelled and cheered at the thought of being reunited with their old friend TV.

"That's *awesome!*" Val whispered, turning to the table with a big smile. "I was starting to go into withdrawal."

"I'm *totally* going into withdrawal," echoed Candace. "My mom and I watch the soaps every day during the summer. I'm, like, thirty hours of TV behind!"

Dr. Steve held up his hands to stop the noise. "All right, calm down, calm down. I'm happy you're so enthusiastic, but there *are* more important things in life than TV, I promise. Tonight, we'll have our campfire as planned. But tomorrow night, we'll all gather in the auditorium to watch the first episode of *Survival Camp*. We'll watch three episodes I've taped this week, and the two more taped episodes next week, and then finally the season finale as it airs! Next Thursday, the series will end and the winner will be chosen. We'll have popcorn and hot chocolate to celebrate. And the next night, we'll have our social."

The excitement level in the hall was still pretty high, so Gaby had to lean in to hear Jenna when she asked, "Who's going with who to the social?"

Each year, Camp Lakeview threw a social for the campers. It was always a hot topic of conversation — especially once the girls started caring about boys, and who would go with who. Everyone looked around at everyone else, but none of the girls seemed to have a ready answer.

"Well, you're going with David, obviously," Nat told Jenna.

"Right." Jenna looked at Alex. "And?"

"I'll go with Adam, I'm sure," Alex said. "He just has to ask me."

"I'll go with Jordan," Brynn added.

"Grace can go with Spence," Gaby announced with a smile. "Right, Grace? Like Priya said, you'd have fun."

Grace looked at Gaby like she thought everyone was

46

playing a big joke on her, but couldn't be sure. "Um, maybe," she replied. "Why are you all—"

"What about you and Simon?" Chelsea asked Nat suddenly, interrupting Grace.

Nat shrugged. "I dunno," she said. "We're just friends. If he wants to go as friends, that's cool."

Everyone was quiet for a minute as the other tables started getting up and heading for the campfire.

"Remember last year?" Tori asked as she stood up and pushed in her chair. "We were all so, like, *nuts* about the social. Remember how we tried to get dates, and make the theme more romantic?"

Brynn snorted. "Right," she said with a laugh. "Well, what can I say? We were boy crazy, I guess. I'm glad we're more mellow now."

"Yeah," Alyssa agreed.

"Yeah," Grace added. But as she looked around at her friends, she sounded a little unsure.


"So what do you think this show is like?" Alex asked as she and her bunkmates lounged in the soft grass near the campfire. The rest of the camp was engrossed in a counsellor's ghost story, but having recently lived through some real-life ghost stories, bunk 5A was uninterested.

"It's cool," replied Tori. "It's like *Survivor* for kids, basically. My dad saw the pilot. One of his clients is the host."

"How does it work?" Gaby asked.

Tori leaned back to look at the stars, speaking in a monotone. "Twelve campers. They pair up differently in every show, and they have to perform a challenge — something to do with surviving in the wilderness that requires teamwork. Each episode, one pair is sent home. Then, at the end, the last two have to defend themselves to the judges, and whoever does the best is the winner." She pushed her long blonde hair back from her face.

"Cool," breathed Val. "It sounds interesting."

"Do they have to build their own shelters?" asked Jenna.

Tori nodded. "Yeah. They get, like, basic supplies. Water. Some PowerBars. But everything else, they have to make."

Jenna wrinkled her nose. "Even toilet paper?"

Tori laughed. "Yeah, even that."

"Who gets to decide who goes home?" Chelsea asked. "The host?"

Tori shook her head. "No, there's a team of judges. Psychiatrists and nature experts and stuff. They review all the footage and decide."

"Do they go right home?" Chelsea asked.

Tori shook her head again. "No. I think they put them in a hotel nearby, then they bring them back for the last episode."

Chelsea looked puzzled. "The people who get kicked off, they come back? Like, they're competing again?"

Gaby scratched a mosquito bite on her ankle and bit her tongue to keep from saying something snarky. *Chelsea never understands anything.*

Tori seemed unbothered though. "No, Chelse. They bring them back to be in the audience when the winner is announced. Once you're out, you're out."

Chelsea still looked confused. "Why don't they just send them home then?" she asked. "If they're not going to be able to win. I'd hate to lose and then just have to sit around doing nothing."

Gaby was getting tired of all these questions. "Because that's the way the show is!" she said. "If you have such a problem with how the game is played, become a TV producer and make your own show!"

Silence fell over the group. Gaby felt her heart sink as she noticed everyone staring at her, stunned. *Uh-oh. I did it again.*

"Jeez, Gaby," Alyssa muttered disapprovingly. "Harsh much?"

"I'm just trying to understand the *game*," Chelsea whined.

"It's easy," Gaby said, trying to make her voice gentler. "Twelve kids. They camp. They get voted out one by one, and then one wins. What's so hard about that?"

"*Actually*," Chelsea replied, sitting up with a big cat-that-ate-the-canary smile, "they get voted out two by two. In *pairs*. Until the very end, when one wins." She smirked and then turned her back on Gaby. "But I wouldn't have understood that if it weren't for all the *stupid* questions."

Gaby felt her face turning red. The other girls were laughing and smiling; once again, she'd made a fool of herself by trying to shut up Chelsea. She couldn't *take* this any more. Chelsea lied and whined and acted dumb, and *still* she managed to come out on top.

"I don't need *you* to explain the stupid game to me," Gaby hissed. "I understand the stupid game. I probably understand it better than you do!" With that, she turned her back on her bunk and tried to take deep breaths. *Calm down, Gaby,* she told herself. *Every time you lose your temper, it all gets ten times worse.*

Candace's voice floated over from the circle. "What do you mean you understand it better than we do?" she asked timidly. "Do you have some kind of connection? Like Tori?"

50

Gaby's breath caught. She'd never meant to imply that she had a connection to the show — of course she didn't. Her dad was an accountant, not some big-time celebrity lawyer like Tori's father. But her bunkmates didn't know that. In fact, they didn't know much of anything about her family.

*Like Tori.* She thought of the way everyone had fallen all over Tori, peppering her with questions and hanging on her answers. Nobody ever accused Tori of being mean or snarky. They all thought she was cool because her dad was so connected to Hollywood.

Gaby turned back around. "I'm...not supposed to talk about it," she said finally.

Nat's eyes widened. "You mean you *do*?" she asked. "Seriously? I thought you were just being a jerk."

Jenna chuckled nervously. "I think what Nat's trying to say is that we're surprised." She glanced over at Nat, who shrugged unapologetically. "Since you didn't say anything before. I mean, what's your connection?"

Gaby blinked. What *was* her connection? "I mean, I'm not supposed to talk about it. Like I said. You know what, just forget I said anything. I don't want to get in trouble with the produc – with *anybody*." Gaby smiled. It was a real smile; she couldn't help it. The way she'd let her voice tremble a little, like she really was nervous? And namechecking the "producers", a term

Tori threw around all the time? *Perfect save.*

Everyone was looking at her with wide-eyed wonder again, like she'd just transformed from a hideous troll into Jake Gyllenhaal right before their eyes. "Seriously?" Val asked with a little smile. "You don't want to get in trouble with the producers?"

*Ten points.* Gaby tried to look uncomfortable. "Let's just change the subject."

"Oh, no," insisted Alex, waving her hand around. "Oh, no no no no no. You're giving us details."

"You can't just leave us hanging," Brynn agreed.

Gaby shook her head. "I can't, really. I shouldn't have said anything." Now she *was* getting a little nervous. She didn't *have* details — there were no details. How was she going to get out of this?

"Maybe you shouldn't have said anything," Priya said, "but *you* opened your big mouth, not us. I don't think we should have to suffer. You have to tell us!"

Gaby didn't say anything. She wondered if she looked as terrified as she felt. Probably not. She was good at hiding things.

"What about tomorrow?" Tori asked after a few seconds. "If you don't want to ruin some surprise, why not wait till tomorrow night, after we've all seen the show? Then we'll already have all our opinions formed and whatever. I mean, you can't ruin the ending for us." She yawned and sat up, circling her knees with her arms.

"Why can't she ruin it?" Chelsea asked, still pouting.

Tori shrugged. "It's live," she said. "The series was all taped. But the finale is live. She can't know who wins, because nobody's won yet."

Gaby felt a rush of relief at this new information. Live! So that meant they couldn't expect her to know anything about what happens, because even if she were connected to the show, she couldn't predict the future. *Gaby*, she thought to herself, *this is the perfect plan. You'll be the centre of attention, and you can be just as surprised as everyone else!*

"All right," she agreed, trying to make a big show of looking hesitant. "I'll tell you tomorrow, after the show. But you can't tell anyone."

"Awesome." Jenna actually smiled at her. Gaby smiled back, and felt a happy glow settling over her. *Awesome*, she thought.

*Now I just have to figure out what my secret is.*

# CHAPTER FOUR

"Hey, congrats on winning the scavenger hunt last night," Grace heard Alyssa telling Spence as she walked into the newspaper room alone.

Grace wasn't entirely sure how she felt about being back in newspaper. All through lunch, the conversation had been about Chelsea, and Cropsy, and what had happened while Grace was in summer school. Grace knew her bunkmates had had an intense time on the overnight, but couldn't they see that the constant retellings only made her feel more left out? Besides that, she was still totally confused about what had happened at lunch yesterday. For some reason, it seemed like everyone was pushing her to admit that she liked Spence, when really, they'd only had one, admittedly nice, conversation.

*Why?* What was the big deal about her liking Spence, or not liking Spence? The obvious answer would be that her friends wanted her to have a boyfriend, but even that…Grace had a weird feeling about it. Something in the way Gaby, Priya and Chelsea had responded seemed *off*. Grace couldn't put her finger on it. And even if they were being totally sincere – what was the big deal about her getting a boyfriend? Did they think she was pathetic on her own or something? Was it because sending her off with some boy would be easier than trying to include her?

If dinner yesterday had never happened, Grace knew she would actually be looking forward to seeing Spence again – Spence *was* funny, and cute, and the work they'd done yesterday had been more fun than she'd expected. But since the conversation at dinner *had* happened, all she could think about was how her friends would react to her getting closer to Spence. And that made her not so excited about the Spence thing. In fact, it kind of made her want to avoid Spence altogether.

"Thanks," Spence was saying, "but we just got lucky, basically. When Adam started wading into the lake to get that coin, I thought he was totally nuts. Who knew we'd have to get wet?"

"We didn't even get that clue," Alyssa admitted. "As soon as Nat realized she'd have to get her clothes wet, she was like, forget it."

Spence laughed. "Yeah, I guess the guys had a little

bit of an advantage. We don't mind getting wet, or slimy, or muddy." He glanced up and saw Grace standing off to the side. "Hey, partner."

Grace felt herself blushing. *Great*, she thought. *I haven't even figured out whether I like him, but thanks to my bunkmates, he's going to see me blushing and think I do.* "Hey," she said, trying to sound unenthused.

"So," Spence said, "I'd say maybe you guys can crash our ice cream party, but I think Adam would freak out. He was very, 'we beat the girls!' about it."

"Not a problem," Alyssa said.

"I'm lactose intolerant," Candace added solemnly.

"Well all right, Debbie Downer," Alyssa said with a little laugh. "Let's go, we have a lot of work to do on our piece today. And I'm sure Spence and Grace are — *busy*." Alyssa gave Grace a quick wink before walking away.

*Great*, Grace thought. *I hope Spence didn't see that.*

But Spence had already turned back to his mountain of notes.

"Remember the 'amfog'," he read from one particularly messy one. He held it up to Grace. "Does that mean anything to you?"

Grace shook her head.

"Right." He pushed his pile of notes away and gestured to some papers on a far table. "I think today, we should sort through these. They're paintings and drawings from the arts and crafts classes. We need to pick two from each division to put in the paper — one from a girl, one from a boy."

Grace nodded without looking at him. She kept her attention on the artwork. "Okay."

Spence lifted up the first one. "Should we go through them together?"

Grace bit her lip. "Um, actually, maybe we should split them up and each go through half," she said. She figured the less time they spent doing anything that might look like "canoodling", the better.

Spence looked confused. "Then how will we pick the best ones?"

Grace shrugged. "We can each pick out our favourites, then we can look at those together."

Spence looked at Grace for a moment without saying anything. She could tell he noticed that she was being less than friendly, and that he was wondering why. But she couldn't tell him. No, it was better to just cool off a little bit, and once the rumours died down, she could be nice again. "Okay," he said finally.

Grace brought her stack of artwork over to a table across the room, careful to avoid eye contact as much as possible. She spread out the paintings and drawings and separated them into girls' and boys' piles. It was harder than she expected to narrow it down to her few favourites, but finally she selected one for each grade level and gender: two watercolours, one of the lake and one of campers playing capture the flag; two pencil drawings, one of a cabin and one of a canoe on the beach; and two bold, colourful acrylic paintings, one of a sunset and one of — well, Grace wasn't sure, actually. She only knew that she liked it.

"That one's cool." She suddenly heard Spence's voice from behind her. "All colour and shape. It kind of reminds me of this dude Kandinsky. They had a show at the Smithsonian a couple of years ago."

"Oh," Grace said. "Well, m—" She cut herself off before she could reply. She was going to say, *Well, maybe someday this kid will have a show in the Smithsonian*. But she realized too late that she was supposed to be *cool* to Spence. *Cool* as in aloof and mysterious — and as in not having random conversations about the artistic talents of third-division boys.

"You were saying?" Spence asked, looking her right in the eye. Grace had to look away. Spence was going to be hard to lie to.

She shook her head. Then she lifted up her finalists. "These," she said simply. She figured Spence would figure out that she meant, *These are the ones I liked best.* The fewer words actually spoken, the better.

"Ohhh-kay," Spence muttered, picking up her choices with a funny look on his face. He carried them across the room, back to the table where he'd been working. "C'mon," he called behind him when Grace didn't immediately follow. She scampered after him.

"What's your choice for third-division girl?" Spence asked. She pointed to the canoe drawing.

"All right," Spence said, still looking suspicious. "You take a vow of silence or something?"

Grace shook her head, confused. "What's that?"

Spence sighed. "Forget it. Just something monks do." He pulled a painting from his pile, a watercolour of dandelions. "Here's mine. Which do we like better?"

Grace looked at the two pieces of artwork for a few seconds, then pointed to the dandelion picture.

Spence glanced at her, shrugged, and then pointed to the canoe picture. "Well, I like that one better. Now what?"

*Now I guess we have to talk to each other,* Grace thought. But she wanted to avoid that as much as possible. She shrugged and looked away, over at Alyssa and Candace, who were hunched over a computer again. "I don't care. You can use yours."

Spence didn't say anything for a minute. He didn't even move or sigh; he just kind of stood there, looking at Grace. Grace closed her eyes and waited for the moment to pass. *Don't turn around, don't turn around.*

"Are you okay?" Spence asked. His voice was warm with concern.

Grace wanted so much just to tell him what was going on. To admit that she was feeling weird about missing the first two weeks of camp, and that she felt like her friends were leaving her out — maybe not on purpose, but still. But she knew if she did, they would end up talking and "canoodling", just like yesterday. And she didn't want to have another dinner conversation like the one last night. "Fine," she said shortly.

"Okay," Spence said with a sigh.

Picture by picture, they went through the rest of the artwork. When it came time to pick the fifth-division pictures, Spence said, "I have to get those from over there," and pointed to a table across the way where a few pictures were still scattered.

"Okay," Grace replied, nervously fingering a corner of a painting. She didn't look as he walked over to the other table and fiddled with the artwork.

After a minute, Spence returned with his arms full of pictures. "Here we go." He put down the pile and stood back, gesturing for Grace to pick up the first one. She lifted a drawing of two girls sitting on a cabin stoop and gasped.

On a drawing-size piece of paper underneath, the words WAS IT SOMETHING I SAID? were spelled out in red block letters. Spence's messy handwriting. Actually it looked more like WAS IT SOMEFING I SAIG?, but Grace decided to let that one go.

She let out a little laugh, and Spence smiled with relief. "Seriously," he said to her. "You seem a little weird today. Is it me?"

Grace took a deep breath. "No," she admitted, "it's not anything you said. It's not anything you did, either. It's just – me being stupid."

Spence didn't laugh, or look at her like she was crazy. He just watched her, patiently, waiting for her to explain what she meant. Grace couldn't put her finger on it, but when she was with Spence, she felt like there was nothing she could say or do that would surprise or offend him – everything she did and everything she said was totally normal, interesting, even cool.

"I guess it started with me missing the first two weeks of camp," Grace went on. "I came back and – it felt like I'd missed so much! There was some crazy camping trip, and half the people I like didn't come back this year...I guess I felt...I mean...I guess I feel... like I don't quite fit in." She sighed and looked at her flip-flops. "Sometimes – like when everyone's having a conversation around me about something I wasn't even

61

here for — I feel like I didn't have to come to camp this year. You know? Like, I could have skipped camp altogether, and nobody would have noticed but me."

Grace kept looking at her toes. They were raggedy and bare — another sign that she hadn't been at camp last session. If she'd been there more than two days, Natalie or Tori would have attacked her and given her the Pedicure To End All Pedicures, with sparkles, French tips and little flower transfers. All the other girls' toes were flawless.

Spence still hadn't said anything.

Just as Grace was deciding that she had said way too much and was putting together a plan to die of embarrassment, he finally said, "That's dumb."

Grace felt her face flush. "I know," she said, feeling her stomach drop. "I'm being totally—"

"*I* would miss you," Spence went on. "I mean, I know we don't know each other well. But I think you're cool."

Grace looked into Spence's eyes. She couldn't believe he was being so nice. "Wow," she said finally. "Thanks."

Spence shrugged. "Don't mention it." He pulled the WAS IT SOMETHING I SAID? note out of the pile and arranged a pine tree painting next to the drawing of the two girls. "I think the girls. What do you think?"

"The girls," Grace agreed.

Spence grabbed the drawing and placed it in the pile of pictures that would appear in the paper. Before grabbing the next two pictures, he flashed Grace the sweetest smile and reached out to touch her shoulder. "*Now* we're getting somewhere," he said.

*Yeah*, thought Grace, as she felt like she was floating up to the ceiling. *Now we are.*


"The first rule of *Survival Camp*—" Dr. Steve began as all the campers gathered in the auditorium that night.

"Is don't talk about *Survival Camp!*" yelled a male voice from the audience.

Dr. Steve didn't look upset, though. He smiled. "Actually, yes," he agreed, "in a way. What I want is for everyone to be quiet and keep their comments to a minimum while the show is playing. Once it's over, we'll bring the lights back up and break off into groups to discuss the episode."

Brynn was off getting one of her *Guys and Dolls* costumes fitted, so she wasn't going to get to watch all of *Survival Camp*. Grace glanced over at Jenna, who was sitting to her left, but Jenna was already looking over at Alex and smiling. Grace turned to her right, where Gaby was sitting, but Gaby was staring straight ahead, chewing on a hunk of her hair, deep in thought.

*Fine,* Grace thought. *Guess I won't have any trouble keeping quiet.*

A huge screen hung over the stage of the auditorium, and the counsellors had rigged up some sort of device that would project the show onto the screen so everyone could watch at once. Grace felt weird watching TV at camp, but then a lot of things about camp this year felt weird, so whatever.

The lights dimmed and a goofy tune played – the intro to the theme song of *Survival Camp*. Soon Grace forgot all about feeling left out, and the weird events of the day, as she became lost in the story of twelve kids who were sent to live in a remote part of Utah and form pairs to set up camp. The cast was comprised of a lot of familiar characters: the bad boy; the would-be rapper; the spoiled girl; the aggressive, insecure guy; the needy drama queen. Grace felt like she knew some of these characters. They reminded her, in small ways, of people she knew back at school.

It was almost a shock when the would-be rapper and the drama queen were voted out, and soon the credits rolled and the lights in the auditorium came back up. Grace and her friends all looked around at one another, smiling and blinking. *"That was so cool,"* mouthed Val. Grace nodded and rubbed her eyes, trying to adjust to the bright light.

"All right," Dr. Steve said, running back up onto the stage. "We're going to break up into discussion groups now. Third division will meet in the mess hall; fourth division in the gym; fifth division stay here."

Grace saw Jenna and Alex smiling at each other when they realized that the discussion group would include girls and boys. Once the younger kids filed out, Belle and the other fifth-division counsellors moved them onto the stage, where they all settled into a circle. Grace caught Spence winking at her. She grinned automatically and winked back.

"So," began Belle, "what did you guys think about the show?"

"I thought it was cool," David said. "And I think it was mighty cool of you to let us watch it."

"Well," Belle replied, looking a little flustered, "great then. But who were some of your favourite contestants? Let's go around and say who we liked the best, and then why."

Grace listened as Adam explained that he liked Kyle, the funny guy; Chelsea admitted that she liked Didi, the drama queen; and so on. The conversation went on to some of the specifics of the camps, the various mistakes different pairs had made, and finally the ending.

"Was anybody surprised by the ending?" asked Hugh, the boys' counsellor.

"I was," said Chelsea. "I totally thought Didi would win."

"I wasn't surprised that she and Jim got voted out," Spence said, "but I *was* surprised they got voted out first."

Belle nodded, looking curious. "Who did you think would get voted out?"

"Jake," Spence replied without hesitation. "That kid was hopeless."

Grace smiled. Jake was a short, skinny kid with big spiky hair. He was allergic to everything, afraid of heights and the dark, and didn't know how to swim. Grace agreed with Spence – she had thought Jake was a goner.

"Well," said Fiona, another counsellor, "why do you think he was allowed to stay? What do you think the judges saw in him?"

Jenna shrugged. "He's a nice enough kid," she suggested. "I mean, he was friendly to everyone."

"And he did everything his partner asked him to do," added Adam. "I mean, the things he *could* do."

"Why do you think they work in pairs?" Belle asked. "I mean, rather than singles."

There was silence for a moment.

"So they can work as a team?" asked Chelsea.

"Yeah," David agreed. "They probably look at

teamwork and stuff." He glanced at Jenna with a knowing expression. *Teamwork*, Grace thought. *Exactly what Dr. Steve thinks we're all so bad at.*

Belle smiled. "So what does that tell us?"

"Teamwork is important!" cried Jenna, giving an exaggerated punch in the air.

Belle sighed. "All right. No need to get sarcastic." She looked at her watch. "Oh! It's ten o'clock already. Okay, guys, remember where we left off. We'll all pay special attention to Jake's progress in tomorrow's episode."

Gradually, everyone started to get up. David and Jenna and Adam and Alex ran over to each other to say a quiet "goodnight". Grace glanced over at Spence, who was already heading towards the doors of the auditorium. He turned around and caught her eye, though, and mouthed a silent *"goodnight"*. Grace smiled and nodded. *"Goodnight,"* she mouthed back.

Soon, all of 5A was assembled and headed back along the path to their cabin. Belle and Clarissa lagged behind, so the girls started discussing the show on their own.

"Jake doesn't have a chance," Jenna hissed in a stage whisper. "I'm sorry, he's probably a really nice guy, but he's no camper. No matter how good at *teamwork* he is."

"Totally," Tori agreed. "I bet he gets voted out next episode. He just has no skills."

Grace turned around to see who was behind her and caught Gaby's eye. Gaby looked annoyed for some reason, and she was still chewing on her hair, totally lost in thought. Right at that moment, Grace remembered Gaby's "big secret". In all the excitement over the show, they'd forgotten to ask her about it.

"So, guys," Gaby announced suddenly, sprinting forward so she was in the middle of the pack. "You're probably wondering about my connection to the show."

Everyone turned around slowly. Their expressions said that no, they hadn't been wondering about her connection to the show, and in fact, they'd forgotten about it completely until she brought it up. Still, they looked curious.

"Oh yeah," said Priya. "So what is it? I totally forgot."

Everyone murmured agreement, gathering around Gaby with expectant looks.

"Do you know someone?" asked Natalie. "Did you, like, go to school with one of those kids?"

Gaby practically beamed. Her face was flushed with excitement as she shook her head. "Not really," she replied. "I mean, kind of. If you want to get technical."

"Technical?" asked Candace. "What do you mean?"

"Tell us!" cried Alex, her eyes bugging out in frustration. "Come on, Gaby. What is it? Just tell us!"

"Well," said Gaby slowly, clearly enjoying keeping them waiting. "You know that Jake kid?"

Tori nodded furiously. "Sure. Jake. What about him?"

Gaby smiled. She looked around at all the faces, clearly enjoying every moment. "Well," she said simply, "he's my brother."

# CHAPTER FIVE

*That's right, he's my brother!* Gaby couldn't keep the huge smile off her face as she realized how *perfect* that was. Only first names were used on the show – so nobody would realize that she and Jake weren't related. Besides, Jake clearly wasn't cut out for camping – he was probably going to be voted out in the next episode. Once he was voted out, Gaby could just say, "Oh, tough luck," and go back to her life as usual. But in the meantime, all eyes were on her – and her bunkmates looked *beyond* impressed that she was related to one of the show's stars.

"Are you *kidding*?" demanded Priya. "Jake is your *brother*? Shut *up*!"

Gaby shook her head. "It's true," she said. "He really is."

"Oh, wow." Val looked concerned. "All that stuff we said about him – I mean, we never would have called him hopeless if we knew he was your brother."

Gaby shrugged. "You know what, I call him 'hopeless' all the time," she ad-libbed. "At home we're always fighting because he's too weak to do this or too scared to do that! I feel like I have to do everything."

Natalie was watching her with a calculating look. "It's interesting," she said, "how you've never mentioned that you have a brother before."

Gaby tried to look puzzled. She racked her brain to try to remember whether she'd ever told her bunkmates she was an only child. *Why would Natalie remember that?* "I haven't? I'm sure I have."

Jenna shook her head. "Actually, no," she said. "For some reason, I thought you were an only child."

Alex nodded. "Me too. I don't know where I got that, though."

Gaby shrugged again and tried to look innocent, directing her words at Natalie. "Oh well. Maybe I don't mention him that much because there's not much to say. His grades aren't that good, and he doesn't play sports or anything." She sighed and shook her head. *Here's where I go for that Academy Award.* "It's sad, really. My parents are always asking him, 'Why can't you be more like Gaby?'"

Gaby thought she heard a snort coming from Grace's direction. But when she turned to look at

71

Grace, Grace was staring up at the stars, totally in her own world.

"Wow," Tori was saying. "This is so crazy, Gaby. I had no idea your *brother* was one of the kids. How did he get cast?"

Gaby thought fast. She always read stories in her mom's entertainment magazines about kids getting "discovered" in parking lots or malls. "We were at the movies," she replied. "This guy came up to us while we were in line to buy popcorn, and he was like, 'I bet you'd be perfect for our new reality show.'" She paused, debating whether or not she should add to that, and then continued. "At first they wanted us both. But then they realized I'd been coming to Camp Lakeview for so long, I'd have an unfair advantage against all the other kids."

Tori looked confused. "Wait a minute, wait a minute. I thought you had to apply to be on the show? When my dad saw the pilot, it came with all the audition tapes of the contestants."

All eyes turned to Gaby. "Right," she chirped. "When the producer found my brother, that's what he wanted him to do. Make an audition tape. And we were still really surprised Jake got chosen, like he said on the show. He's not really good at camping, or hiking — or anything, really."

"Huh," Natalie murmured. She didn't have a challenging look on her face any more — but she still didn't look convinced. She turned and started heading towards the cabin, and all the girls followed.

"What were you going to do if we didn't get to watch the show?" Tori asked. "If I knew my brother was competing in this huge reality show and I was missing it, I'd freak."

"My mom's recording it for me," Gaby replied. "Besides, we'll all be really surprised if he wins. So it wasn't a big deal for me to miss."

"Yeah, just your brother on national television," Jenna piped up. "If Adam was on TV, he'd tie us to the couch and force us to watch the whole thing. But I guess Jake's not like that."

"No," Gaby agreed. "He kind of does what I tell him."

Alex smirked. "That, I totally believe."

The girls heard footsteps behind them, and Gaby turned around to see Belle and Clarissa running to catch up. "Guys," she hissed, "Ix-nay on the ow-shay alk-tay. Seriously, I'm not supposed to tell anyone. So don't let Belle hear."

"No problem," Val said. "We'll keep your secret. I can't wait to see how your bro does!"

Gaby grinned as Belle and Clarissa joined them. *Neither can I*, she thought. *Neither can I.*

73

"I can't *believe*," Priya whispered in Gaby's ear as they walked to campfire a couple of nights later, "that Jake is still on!"

"Neither can I," Gaby replied honestly. They'd watched the third episode of *Survival Camp* just now and, amazingly enough, Jake was still on. That caused just a tiny twinge of anxiety in the pit of Gaby's stomach — what if Jake lasted all the way to the end? How would she explain his winning? But deep down, she knew that was still extremely unlikely. The other kids had mastered the arts of whittling, fishing and shelter building. Jake was still nice to everybody, but he wasn't *good* at anything, and sooner or later that had to come back to haunt him.

Gaby and her bunkmates settled in a grassy area a little way back from the campfire. Belle had stayed in the auditorium to get some materials for the next day's nature hunt, and Clarissa was talking to a CIT for the boys named Justin. Priya looked around at the lack of counsellors and then back to Gaby. "There's no one here," she stage-whispered. "Can we talk about Jake and the show?"

Gaby smiled. It seemed like everything had changed in just the short amount of time since she let her bunk in on her "secret". Every time they had an unattended minute now, the girls were pumping her for information and insights about Jake. The *Guys and Dolls* rehearsals were going really well – earlier today, Brynn had complimented Gaby on her "body language". And even better, Chelsea hadn't been going on as much about her nightmares. *Finally* things in bunk 5A seemed to be headed in the right direction.

"Sure," Gaby replied with an indulgent shrug. "I mean, if you guys really want to."

"We do!" insisted Priya.

"I have a question," Natalie spoke up. "You've been coming to Camp Lakeview for years now. Don't you tell Jake about any of the stuff we do here? He acted like he'd never heard of a trust fall tonight."

Gaby opened her mouth to speak, but fell silent for a minute. *Why?* She asked herself. There had to be a plausible explanation. She'd been able to make one up for everything else. "Of course I tell him about that stuff," she replied. "But brothers never listen. He's all like, 'Whatever – you're blocking the TV.'"

Natalie seemed to accept this. She nodded and glanced away. "Well, it's good he finally did the trust fall," she suggested. "I bet that's what kept him from being voted off."

"What are you going to do if he wins, Gaby?" Val

asked from the other side of the circle. "You get a trip to Australia! Can you imagine?"

"I've always wanted to go to Australia," Brynn said. "I want to see the Sydney Opera House, and go camping in the outback."

"Maybe you'll meet Crocodile Dundee," Alyssa suggested.

"Uh, yeah," Tori said with a laugh, "because no one's made a new movie since 1986. Alyssa, seriously: think Nicole Kidman and Hugh Jackman. You need a Netflix subscription."

Alyssa just smiled.

Gaby started thinking about going to Australia – the accents! The kangaroos! – before she realized that there wasn't the slightest chance of that ever happening. She wondered briefly who the real Jake was. Could he be persuaded to pretend Gaby was his sister? But then she pushed that thought away.

"Anyway," she said, "it's not happening. Trust me, my brother will screw up and get voted off."

"Have you heard from your parents?" Jenna asked. "They must be freaking out."

"Uh, yeah." Actually, Gaby hadn't heard from her parents since they'd e-mailed back and forth a couple of times at the beginning of camp. At the moment, they were at an accountants' convention in Nashua, an hour or so from camp. "I got an e-mail from them on Sunday. They're thrilled."

"I'll bet," Alex said. Everyone was quiet for a moment, enjoying the crackle of the campfire. Gaby took a deep breath of the night air and let out a contented sigh. She couldn't remember the last time she'd felt this good.

Suddenly Chelsea shot up from where she'd been lying back in the grass. "Did you guys hear that?!"

Gaby felt her stomach muscles tighten. *Oh, no*, she thought, biting her tongue to keep from saying anything. *Not Chelsea's House of Horror again.*

Brynn looked over at Chelsea's "afraid" face, looking sympathetic and wary at the same time. "What is it, Chelse?"

Chelsea looked around, squinting to search the dark woods. "I just – maybe I'm imagining things. I heard something that sounded like a moan."

Gaby turned around so no one would see her roll her eyes.

"I didn't hear anything," Alyssa said.

"*Oh no!*" Chelsea jumped, gathering her hoodie around her like a security blanket. "There it was again! Hear it?"

Gaby strained her ears to hear. Waaayyy in the distance, she heard a faint *woooo*...the trees rustling in the wind.

77

"Chelsea," Alex said, "I think that's the wind."

Chelsea was motionless for a moment, casting her eyes to the side and listening with all her might. Finally she relaxed. "Wow, guys," she said with a sigh. "Sorry about that. It just reminded me of the sound Cropsy made when he was running after me."

Gaby felt her heart thumping hard with frustration. *No*, she thought. *Not tonight. Chelsea is not going to steal my spotlight with this tonight.*

"*Everything* reminds you of Cropsy!" she cried, surprising even herself with the force of her words. "The shape of the trees. The light. The wind! The other morning you said your *pancakes* reminded you of Cropsy's eyes staring right at you! You need to get over it, Chelsea! For your sake and everyone else's."

Chelsea's mouth hung open as she stared at Gaby. Everything fell silent. Even the wind, it seemed, was too taken aback by Gaby's outburst to continue moaning in the trees. All the bunkmates just stared, looking from Gaby, to Chelsea, to one another with stunned expressions.

*Now I've done it*, Gaby scolded herself. *That was stupid. Any goodwill I built up with the Jake thing is gone. Now I'm just the mean girl again.*

"I can't believe you just said that to me," Chelsea said finally, finding her voice. "I was *really scared* when we went camping in the woods! I can't help it if some stuff still scares me!"

"You can't help it," Candace agreed. "It's true, Gaby — that was kind of mean."

Gaby felt her stomach sink.

But then Alex cleared her throat. "Actually," she said quietly, "I wouldn't have put it exactly like that, Chelse, but maybe it *is* time for you to get over what happened in the woods and stop looking for reasons to be scared all the time."

Chelsea stared at Alex in amazement. She looked surprised, and a little hurt, too.

"Yeah," Valerie agreed. "Not to be mean, but it *has* been almost two weeks, Chelsea. I know you're scared, but maybe you'd have more fun if you focused on the *now*, not what happened last session."

"Yeah," said Jenna softly. "I was going to say something to you, Chelsea, but I didn't know how. If you're really that scared, maybe you should talk to a counsellor or something."

Chelsea didn't say anything. She closed her mouth tight and looked off to the side, ignoring them all. But Gaby could see the message had hit home.

Soon Brynn started talking about the *Guys and Dolls* rehearsals, and she was even nice enough to point out how great Gaby had been in a scene today, which Priya agreed with. Gaby smiled and was able to be genuinely gracious as her bunkmates complimented her. She settled back on her elbows and looked at the stars.

*Everything's coming up Gaby — and I have Jake to thank.*

# CHAPTER SIX

"What about this one?"

Spence was holding up a sassafras leaf with just the tiny hint of a smile.

"Oooh, I love sassafras," Grace said, moving closer. "I love the little polka dots on the leaves. And I love that they smell like root beer."

"Seriously?"

"Seriously." Grace grabbed the leaf out of Spence's hand and waved it under her nose. "Mmm. I could really go for a root beer float right about now."

Spence grabbed the leaf and took a whiff. "Wow. How cool is that? But let's not ignore the more important question."

Grace scrunched up her eyebrows. "Which is?"

Spence smiled, dangling the leaf by its stem. "Will this leaf be good for deck-paging?"

Grace couldn't help laughing. "Spence. Say it with me. *Day-coo-paaj*. Découpage."

Spence shrugged. "Right, whatever. Deck-paaj."

"You should probably learn to say it if we're going to put the craft in the newspaper."

Spence gave her a funny look. "Why? I can spell it, and that's all that matters. That's the great thing about journalism."

Grace laughed. "But what if you want to bring up découpaging in conversation some day?"

"I find that extremely unlikely." Spence placed the leaf carefully in a folder, then glanced at his watch. "Ooh, we should get going. I think we have enough leaves to cover the picture frame. We have just enough time to get these back to the newspaper room and head to dinner. We can probably finish the craft tomorrow."

"All right."

Spence started walking the rocky path back to the building where the newspaper elective met, and Grace easily fell into step behind him. Ever since they'd had the conversation about Grace feeling weird this year, things had been so *easy* between them. In fact, Grace felt like these days, Spence was even easier to talk to than her bunkmates. He made her laugh, was totally interested in what she had to say, and better still, he never brought up the camping trip or made her feel weird about all the things she had missed.

Not that they had started "canoodling", or whatever Gaby would call it. In fact, Spence had never said anything directly romantic to Grace. She knew he liked her a lot, but whether that was as a friend or something more, she wasn't sure. And actually, for now, that was just fine with her.

Spence and Grace ducked into the newspaper room after it had already half cleared out.

"People must be hungry today," Spence observed.

"It's pizza night," Grace replied. "You know what that means. Crazy stampede into the mess hall."

"Right, everyone's camping out for their right to pepperoni." Spence dropped the folder of leaves among his pile of notes on the desk. "Mission accomplished! Let's go get in the pepperoni line."

"Um, Spence," Grace said, grabbing the folder and walking over to place it carefully inside the cubby with her name on it, "maybe we should put this somewhere safe, so we don't have to leaf-hunt again tomorrow."

Spence wore an expression of mock outrage. "Are you calling me disorganized?"

Grace just looked him up and down. "Didn't you have a notebook when we went into the woods?"

He glanced down at his hands, then reached into his

pockets. "D'oh!" he cried. "You think I left it on that rock we were sitting on? Or down by the lake?"

Grace smiled. "I honestly have no idea."

"Oh, well." Spence stopped searching his pockets and sighed. "At least it didn't have anything important in it. And it's not supposed to rain or anything, right?"

Grace shook her head. "Not according to the weather board."

"Then I can get it tomorrow." Spence pushed up his glasses on his nose and grandly gestured to the doorway. "Shall we?"

Grinning, Grace walked around him and out the door. The sun was going down, and a cool breeze blew off the lake as the two of them headed towards the mess hall.

"Tomorrow," Spence said, "that picture frame will not know what hit it."

"I know," Grace replied enthusiastically. "Do you think it has any idea that it's about to become a great work of art?"

Spence nodded solemnly. "A masterpiece of the modern world."

"The Met will want to do an exhibit on us."

"And the pièce de résistance?" Spence asked. He reached into his pocket and pulled out a tiny digital camera. Holding it up towards the sky, he threw an arm around Grace and pulled her close to him. "Smile!"

Grace smiled. It wasn't hard.

He clicked the button, then put down the camera and flipped it over to look at the LED screen. Grace and Spence smiled up from the picture, looking happier than Grace had felt since she got to camp.

"Perfect," said Grace. "The perfect picture for the perfect frame."

"I'll print it out tonight," Spence promised. Laughing voices were approaching, and he looked down the path. "Oh, look. It's your posse."

Grace felt a twinge of disappointment at the news that her friends were approaching. Not that she wasn't happy to see them – she just wasn't sure, right at that moment, that she wanted to share Spence with them. Soon she could make out Gaby's voice, then Chelsea's and Priya's.

"Heeeeey guys!" Gaby called in a playful voice. "Spence and Grace! What have you been up to?"

Spence shrugged and dropped his camera back in his pocket as the threesome surrounded them. Grace said a quick "hi" to each of her friends, but she couldn't help noticing that they weren't actually looking at her. They only glanced at her quickly before fixing their gaze on Spence.

"Nothing much," Spence replied. "Talking. Chillin'. Making masterpieces. You guys know how it is."

Priya and Chelsea erupted in giggles. Grace wasn't even sure why – did they understand the joke? But then Chelsea gave a blinding smile and touched Spence on the arm.

"You're always making masterpieces, Spence," she said in a flirty voice. "It must be hard to be so talented."

Grace was feeling annoyed about this whole conversation. What had happened to her friends? They were acting like idiots. If they stopped to think about it, they would have *known* Spence wouldn't be impressed by this kind of stupid act. He wasn't the type. He was more...

But then Grace noticed that Spence was grinning. "Right," he agreed. "I *am* ahead of my time."

Giggles all around. Grace was suddenly tempted to flee the scene and get in the pizza line. The doors hadn't opened yet, though, and the rest of 5A was MIA. Besides – Grace was hesitant to admit this even to herself – a big part of her wanted to stick around and see what happened. Was Spence really impressed by all this flirty stuff? Did he view her as just a friend, while he was crushing on Priya or Chelsea or Gaby? Was *that* why everyone had been so weird about Grace and Spence hanging out together?

"Well, you've found the perfect partner in crime," Priya said, glancing at Grace with a quick smile. "You and Grace seem to be having a good time...*hanging out* together."

Priya's eyes jumped back to Spence as she searched his face — looking, it seemed to Grace, for some kind of sign that their "hanging out" was more than just hanging out. Spence didn't seem to get that, though.

"Yeah," he replied, pushing back his light blond hair. "Grace is an awesome friend."

*Friend.* So there it was. Spence didn't like her as anything more. Grace was surprised not to feel immediately crushed. It was more like she didn't know how to feel. She waited to see which of her friends Spence would flirt back with first.

Priya smiled. "So," she said.

"So," Chelsea repeated.

"*So,*" Gaby broke in pointedly, "do you have a date to the social yet, Spence? Popular guy like you, I bet you do."

Priya bit her lip and Chelsea started fiddling with the hem of her T-shirt. Both of them glanced at Spence out of the corners of their eyes.

"Well," said Spence, glancing towards the mess hall crowd, "actually, I don't. I've been kind of lazy this year. But the truth is I have someone in mind." He looked at all the girls and smiled. "And she's standing right here."

"*Really?*" asked Gaby, twirling her hair. "Well, there are definitely some great ladies standing right...*here.*"

Gaby gestured right to Priya and Chelsea, totally ignoring Grace. *Thanks, Gaby.*

"Who could it be?" Chelsea asked, trying to sound casual, but her voice was a little too high and wobbly.

"That's very interesting," Priya added, winking at Grace. "Well, are you going to tell us who it is, Spence? Or are you going to let us die of suspense?"

Spence pushed his glasses up on his nose again, then put his hands in his pockets. He glanced at the line for the mess hall again. He seemed totally unaware of the urgency in the girls' voices.

"Okay," he said finally.

But then he did something unexpected. He turned away from Priya, Chelsea and Gaby, and turned right to Grace.

"This isn't exactly how I planned to ask you," he admitted. "But do you want to be my date for the social, Grace?"

Grace couldn't stop the huge smile from breaking out on her face. "Yeah!" she cried happily. It was only then, after she'd agreed, that she saw Priya and Chelsea deflate a little, and Gaby watching her and Spence curiously.

Before Grace could react further, the dinner bell rang and chaos broke out.

"Great!" Spence said. "Not to be rude, girls, but I have to make a break for the pepperoni." Before any of them could say another word, he was gone, sprinting for the mess hall doors.

"Wow," said Priya after a moment.

"Wow," agreed Chelsea.

"*Wow*," Gaby finished. Grace felt as if Gaby was studying her like someone might study a strange but fascinating insect.

If only Grace knew what to do. She was happier than happy to be going to the social with Spence, her new favourite boy person at camp, but she couldn't shake the feeling that something weird had just happened.

"So," she said finally. "Who's hungry for pizza?"

Once they met up with the other girls in 5A and sat down to dinner, things seemed to get a little more normal. They all made a big deal of Grace and Spence going to the social together, of course — especially Brynn, who was thrilled that she and Grace would both have dates. But the weird feeling Grace had had before they went into the mess hall was gone. Priya and Chelsea seemed a little quiet at dinner, but Grace told herself that was probably just a coincidence.

There was no *Survival Camp* episode that night, so after dinner, everyone except Brynn marched to campfire, while Brynn headed to a special rehearsal for leads. Grace was really beginning to miss Brynn. *Oh well*, she told herself. *Once the play's over, things will go back to normal.*

After a few songs, Grace noticed Priya, Chelsea and Gaby all deep in conversation a few metres away. She decided to walk over. She'd gotten kind of a weird feeling before dinner – maybe if she just hung out with them a little, she could get rid of it...

The three of them were speaking softly when Grace approached. She could just barely make out a few of the words Priya was saying.

"...such a *flirt*," Priya was saying. "I mean, who knows? Who knows if he really—" Suddenly she looked up and saw Grace walking over. Her voice went back up to normal volume and she hastily smiled. "Hey, Grace!"

"Hey," Grace replied cautiously. Why would Priya cut off what she was saying like that? What had she missed? "What are you guys talking about?"

"Nothing," Gaby replied quickly.

But Priya gave her a *look* and turned back to Grace with a smile. "We were talking about the social," Priya replied. "And what a dry spell we're all having with boys...except for you!"

Priya's smile widened, but there was something weird about it — it was a little too big and a little too fast. She was the only one smiling, too. Gaby was watching Grace with an indifferent look, and Chelsea was scowling.

"Well," Grace said hesitantly, sitting down, "I'm sure you guys will find people to go with, if you want to. You're all so awesome!"

Priya's eyes warmed and she smiled a genuine smile. "Thanks, Grace."

"So..." Grace went on. She still wanted to know who Priya was talking about before. "Who's a big flirt? You were saying something when I walked up."

Chelsea coughed suddenly and looked away. Priya's smile left her face and she started to look a little nervous. "Who was I talking about? Um..."

"David," Gaby interrupted loudly.

Grace furrowed her eyebrows. That didn't make sense. "David? He seems pretty happy with Jenna. I don't think he's that flirty."

Gaby shrugged. "We meant *before* Jenna."

"You mean when he was with Sarah?" Grace was totally confused.

Priya sighed. She shot Gaby an annoyed look.

"*Actually,*" she admitted, "we weren't talking about David. We were talking about Spence."

Grace looked back at Priya, surprised. She knew she must look hurt. *Why did you lie then?* "Oh. Okay." But then she thought about it. *If Spence is a big flirt...what does that say about him and me?* "You think Spence is a flirt?"

Chelsea rolled her eyes. "It's not what we *think*, Grace. It's the truth. Spence flirted with Priya last summer, then he flirted with me at the beginning of camp. He was flirting with *all* of us before dinner. Didn't you notice?"

Grace bit her lip. *Yeah.* She'd noticed Spence puffing up a little, responding to all the attention. But she'd forgotten about all of that when he'd asked her to the social. "I guess." She paused, realizing that all three girls were looking at her funny – like they had just told her something hugely embarrassing, like that her underwear was showing. "What? Do you..." It hit her all at once. Her stomach dropped. "You think he doesn't really like me, then? He just flirts with me in newspaper because he flirts with everyone?"

Priya reached out and touched Grace's shoulder. "No, no, no. That's not what we were saying. How could he not like you? You're awesome!"

But Grace wasn't convinced. She felt her face getting hot.

Gaby leaned in. "It's just..." she began, then bit her lip. "Spence liked Priya for a long time, and Chelsea too. They've had this *thing* started for a while now. So why would he..."

Gaby didn't finish because Priya shot her a look of death. "That's not what I was saying."

Grace watched hopefully as Priya turned around and met her eyes. Priya looked concerned, but also worried – like she had something more to say.

"Grace," she said gently. "All I was saying is, Spence can be really flirty, and he just likes girls. So sometimes... you know, when a guy has a personality like that...it can be hard to tell who he really likes. That's all I'm saying."

That didn't make Grace feel better at all. She looked at Gaby and Chelsea, who were both looking at her with *Well, duh* expressions. She blinked to clear her eyes, which had started to water.

"You don't think Spence could actually *like* me," she said coldly. And as soon as she said it, the reality of the words hit her – her friends didn't think she was good enough for Spence to really like. *Why?*

Priya bit her lip. "No," she said. "No, I mean – that's not what I—"

"Why not?" Grace asked, and she was embarrassed to hear her voice crack. "Spence and I get along *great*, and he really *listens* to me. He doesn't always talk about

93

stuff that happened before I got here. He thinks I'm smart and funny."

Priya looked hurt. "You *are*—"

But Grace was already standing up. "I just don't get why everyone else who goes out with a guy is girlfriend material, but me, no, oh no, he must just be *flirting* with Grace!"

Gaby sighed. "Get a grip, Grace. You're totally freaking out."

"No," Grace said, shaking her head as she looked from Priya to Chelsea. "He likes me. Not you. I'm sorry, but that's the way it is."

Grace turned and walked away, trembling with anger and hurt. *How could they say that?* she wondered. *I know Spence likes me.* She replayed all their conversations in newspaper, and remembered the way he looked at her, so serious and interested. She thought of the way he laughed at her jokes and made her feel like the only person in the room. It was special – and it was different from the way any other guy had ever treated her.

Grace walked away from her friends, all of her friends. Only Priya and Chelsea and Gaby had been involved in the conversation, but who knew what everyone else thought? Maybe this was what had made everyone act so strangely at dinner the other night – they thought Spence was flirting with Grace, and they wanted to make her feel special, even though they thought she wasn't. *They must think I'm a total loser,* Grace thought, cringing when she remembered the sympathy in Priya's eyes. *Why else would they think he might not really like me?*

*I really wish Brynn were here now.* Brynn would know how to make her feel better. But with Brynn rehearsing practically all the time, Grace was feeling more left out than ever.

Grace's mind was still racing when she charged into the small circle where 5G sat, loading up sticks with marshmallows.

"Hey," she said, crossing the circle and stopping right in front of Spence.

"Hey," Spence replied. If he was surprised to see her, or if he noticed the hurt in her eyes, or if he just found it weird that she would charge right over to him in front of all his friends during campfire, he didn't say anything. Instead he popped a marshmallow off the top of his stick and offered it to her. "Marshmallow?"

Grace reached out and popped the marshmallow in her mouth. The gooey sweetness soothed her, and she was able to blink away the tears burning behind her eyes and take a deep breath. *He offered me a marshmallow. That means he must like me.*

"Thanks," she said and plopped down beside him.

\* \* \*

It was bedtime when Grace returned to her bunkmates. She'd stayed with Spence's bunk for an hour, enjoying their raunchy jokes and endless teasing, and the warm feeling of Spence sitting next to her, every once in a while reaching over to touch her shoulder. When it was time to head back to their cabins, Spence casually took Grace's hand and walked with her to where 5A was sitting, which happened to be on the way back to his cabin.

"See you tomorrow," he said, and gave her hand a little squeeze.

"See you tomorrow," she echoed.

All of 5A seemed to be watching Grace as they gathered up their things and stood. Most of the girls looked surprised – like this Grace, the Grace who took off to hang out with a boy and then held hands with him in front of everybody, wasn't the Grace they knew. But Priya looked upset, and Chelsea and Gaby seemed to be avoiding her eyes.

Grace caught Priya's eye as they began walking back to the cabin. For a second, Priya looked at Grace, her dark eyes wide and searching. But Grace quickly looked away.

# CHAPTER SEVEN

"Tonight's outcasts are..."

Gaby held her breath. She was staring straight at the huge projection screen, chewing on her hair. *Jake,* she thought. *Jake, Jake, Jake. Please. Just let him be voted out tonight.*

"Erica and Anthony."

Gaby let out a huge breath. *Erica?* And *Anthony?* Okay, Erica could be hard to get along with, and their shelter had flooded because they built it too close to a river. But in this episode alone, Jake had burned his partner's dinner, built a latrine next to a hornet's nest, and accidentally dropped his own sleeping bag into the lake. *Clearly* he was unfit for survival camp! Granted... he *had* taught himself how to gut and clean a fish, and how to bait a hook, which enabled his partner to catch three whole fish that Jake prepared perfectly – until he burned them. And in spite of all his dumb mistakes, his partner had praised him — said he was a "fantastic team player".

*Whatever.* Gaby sighed. She felt so frustrated with him, it was almost like he really *was* her brother.

The theme music started up again as the credits rolled, and the lights in the auditorium came back up. Gaby just shook her head. It was official now: Jake was in the final four.

"Wow!" Val whispered, reaching over to grab Gaby's elbow. "You must be *so* psyched! Jake has a one in four chance to win!"

Gaby realized she probably looked horrified, and rushed to put on an "excited" expression. "Yeah. Right. Wow!"

"Do you really think he'll win?" Priya whispered from the other side of Val. "Did you and your parents talk about what you'd do?"

Gaby tried to think fast. If Jake actually *won* — if she was just that unlucky — how would she react? What would the actual sister of a reality show winner do? She had no idea. No one she knew had ever been on television; nobody she knew even *knew* someone who had been on television, except Natalie and Tori, of course. But she knew the winner would be getting a trip to Australia for his whole family that left the *day* after the finale. Either Gaby had to think of some reason she wasn't going — or she would have to "leave" to "go to Australia".

Gaby's stomach clenched. The finale aired the next night. She didn't have nearly enough time to come up with a plan.

"Gaby?" Priya asked with a frown. "Are you okay?"

Gaby shook her head to clear it. "Yeah, I'm fine. Just so excited, you know? My parents are actually at a conference in Nashua, so if he wins I'm supposed to call my mom right away and she'll pick me up. Then we'll drive to New York to meet my dad and Jake. So, you know, that's what I'll do."

Val grinned. "This is *so* cool."

*Right*, Gaby thought. *So cool I'm shaking.*

During siesta the next day, Gaby lay on her bunk and stared at the ceiling. She should have been sleeping — she'd stayed up nearly the whole night before trying to come up with a plan in case Jake won — but there was no way she could sleep with the *Survival Camp* finale only six hours away.

She glanced out the window. Outside, she saw Grace sitting on a rock, painting her toenails. A few of the other girls were trying to nap, like Gaby, but most of them were reading, playing cards, or chatting in quiet conversations. And Brynn was off rehearsing again, as usual. She was constantly rehearsing alone with David — a non-stop reminder that Gaby's role was *not* the lead.

Grace was one of the only non-nappers who wasn't talking to anyone. She still seemed pretty upset about the whole Spence conversation. Gaby felt a little guilty, but then, everything that was said was true, wasn't it? Spence *was* a big flirt. And wasn't it better for Grace to know that now, before next week came and he started flirting with someone *else*?

The funny thing about all of the Spence-related drama was that Gaby, Priya and, yes, *Chelsea* had suddenly all become BFF. Gaby never expected to enjoy Chelsea's company this much — but then, she hadn't mentioned nightmares or flashbacks since that night at campfire when Gaby had called her out. At first they didn't talk much about Grace and Spence — they came up every once in a while, but they never dominated the conversation. Lately, though, Spence seemed to be all Priya and Chelsea thought about. They both claimed they were over him, just interested in his well-being or something. But ever since he'd asked Grace to the social, they'd been kind of quiet and mopey. Yesterday Priya had revealed that even though she didn't like Spence any more, it was a little sketchy of Grace to go out with him. "If it were me," Priya had whispered at the campfire before Grace had come up, "I would stay away awhile, just to respect the other person's feelings."

Gaby had totally agreed.

With that thought, Gaby sat up and dangled her legs over the edge of her mattress. *Looks like I'm not sleeping,* Gaby thought. *I might as well try to do some damage control.*

Slipping on her sparkly pink flip-flops, Gaby quietly opened the cabin door and slipped out. Grace was carefully swishing the brush over her big toe, totally oblivious. Gaby noted, as she got closer, that Grace's toes looked awful. They were all smeary and uneven — nothing like the perfect pedicures the rest of the bunk had gotten from Tori before Grace had arrived.

"Hey," Gaby said casually, dropping down next to Grace.

Grace jumped, making an even bigger smear on her toenail. "Hey," she said. She didn't exactly look happy to see Gaby.

Gaby ignored that and put on her biggest smile. "I can't sleep so I thought I'd come out here and keep you company. What's up?"

Grace looked at her like she was nuts. "What's up?" she asked. "Well, you and Priya and Chelsea seem to think there's no way Spence could like me. Thanks for that, by the way."

Gaby sighed and rolled her eyes. "You're so *sensitive*, Grace," she chided. "We didn't mean to hurt your feelings or whatever. It's just...Spence *is* a flirt. It has nothing to do with how lovable you are. You just don't know what you're getting into."

Grace shrugged, still not impressed. "Well, he *does* like me. I don't get why that's such a big deal."

Gaby shook her head. "Fine, Grace. Seriously, we never meant to hurt your feelings. Let's not let this ruin our friendship."

Grace looked sceptical. "Okay, I guess."

"Great." Gaby put her hands in her lap and watched Grace try to draw a little flower on her toenail with pink polish. She was hopeless. It looked more like a squished frog. "So," Gaby said casually. "What *is* up with you and Spence? Tell me about it."

Grace's shoulders tensed up. "Why are you asking?"

Gaby shrugged. "What do you mean, why am I asking? We're friends, right? Friends catch up with each other."

Grace turned away and wiped away the pink flower-frog, smearing the candy-pink colour over her purple toenail. "It's weird," she said, still not looking at Gaby. "I have this funny feeling you're just asking me about Spence so you can turn around and tell Priya and Chelsea."

"What!" Gaby tried to look shocked, even though that was exactly what she'd been planning. Priya and Chelsea loved talking about Spence so much — they'd be psyched if she came back with new information.

"Look." Grace screwed the top back on the nail polish bottle and turned to face Gaby again. "Spence and I like each other, but we're just hanging out. No canoodling. No kissing. No big romance."

Gaby smirked. "That's not what it looks like to me."

Grace shrugged. "Well, that's what it *is*." She paused. "I know something's going on, Gaby. There's something weird happening with Priya and Chelsea. Why don't you just tell me what it is already, so I can have all the info?"

Gaby was quiet for a moment. It didn't surprise her that Grace knew there was something up, but it *did* surprise her that Grace was bold enough to demand the info from her, point-blank. Grace had changed a lot since their first summer. Gaby scratched a mosquito bite, deciding whether or not to tell her.

"They like him," she said finally. "Priya and Chelsea. You know he liked Priya last year."

"Yeah," agreed Grace. "*Last* year."

"And then when we first got to camp, he and Chelsea were flirting a little bit."

Grace nodded. "Okay. Yeah, she said that last night."

"But then we went on the whole camping trip, and everyone got scared and everyone's thinking sort of changed," Gaby went on. "After that, everyone was all about friendship all the time. So Priya and Chelsea had been kind of fighting over Spence, but they decided to stop. They didn't want to ruin their friendship over a guy. They called him 'neutral territory'."

Grace sighed. "'Neutral territory'?" she repeated.

"Yeah." Gaby looked at Grace. "So *of course* they still like him. And when you guys started hanging out, well, they kind of got jealous. But they won't admit they're jealous, 'cause they're not supposed to like him."

"Right," said Grace. She wasn't looking at Gaby any more. She stared off into the woods, looking pensive.

"I think you should just not get too into him, Grace," she said, looking down at her toes. "He liked both of them first. And he *does* flirt with everyone. No offence."

Grace seemed to think this over. She didn't look angry or immediately try to defend herself, like Gaby had expected. Instead, she slowly stood up.

"Thanks for the info, Gaby," Grace said, turning around and heading for the woods. "I'm going to go for a walk. Alone. I'll see you later."

Gaby sat and watched Grace take off into the trees. She wondered what Grace was going to do about the Spence thing. But she quickly stood up and walked back into the cabin to try to get some rest. *I can't worry too much about Grace — I have my own problems.*

"No way," Priya whispered, grabbing Gaby's hand on the armrest and squeezing it. "No *way!*"

*My thoughts exactly,* Gaby thought. Onscreen, an ad for some new car played, with cheerful music about driving around the country and feeling carefree. Gaby had never felt less carefree in her whole life. Jake, her imaginary brother, was in the final two. And once this commercial break was over, the winner would be chosen.

It was probably a good thing that Gaby was so tense and nervous: at least she'd look excited to her bunkmates. They kept leaning over to catch her eye, bugging their eyes out and mouthing, *"Wow!"* Gaby couldn't believe it had gotten to this point. Even last night, during the worst of her night-long freak-out, she'd thought the odds of Jake actually *winning* were pretty slim. He was well liked by his partners — but he was so much *weaker* than they were! Surely the judges would eventually catch on. And besides, as part of the final four, he had only a twenty-five per cent chance.

Which gave Gaby this terrible feeling in the pit of her stomach.

The guitar riff of the cheesy theme song came back up, and the show replayed the last few seconds before the commercial break:

"Haley," intoned the stone-faced host, "you are... going home."

Haley, a chubby girl with dyed platinum-blonde hair, looked crushed. Jake and the other finalist, Deborah, turned to each other and shrieked, hugging and jumping up and down.

"That means..." The host continued. It seemed like he took a thirty-second break between each word, drawing the suspense out as long as possible. "Jake... and...Deborah...you...are...the...FINAL...TWO!"

Now it was a fifty per cent chance.

All the campers cheered. The nightly conversations had shown that almost everybody liked Deborah and picked her to win; Jake, while not the strongest, was still better than that conniving Haley.

"You will have one minute to make a last speech to the judges," the host went on, returning to a normal pace. "Then, the winner of *Survival Camp* will be chosen."

Gaby took a deep breath. *Deborah can still win. Deborah can still win.* She tried to talk herself down as Deborah made her speech, all about the spirit of competition and her superior skills.

*Right on*, Gaby thought, crossing her fingers hard. *You tell 'em, sister.*

But then Jake got up. He said the win would mean a lot to his family, his parents and — *say you have a sister, say you have a sister* — sister and little brother. He went on to talk about everything he had learned over the course of the competition, not just physical skills, but mental skills too, like courage and the value of teamwork.

Gaby sighed.

*This is so cheesy*, Gaby thought. *The judges will never go for this.*

"Thank you," said the host solemnly. "The judges will now deliberate."

Dramatic music played as the camera panned over the judges, Jake and Deborah, the host, and then the judges again. Gaby was seriously worried that she might have a heart attack before the winner was announced. *I guess that would solve my problem*, she thought, *but I'd kind of like to live to see what happens.*

Thirty seconds and another commercial break later, Jake and Deborah were standing up on a platform, looking as nervous as Gaby felt.

"The...winner...of...*Survival...Camp*," the host announced, "is..."

Suddenly Deborah's half of the platform sank down, while Jake's raised up, and fireworks shot off behind them.

"JAAAAAAAAAAKE!!!"

Gaby's mouth dropped open. *This can't be happening. This can't be happening.*

Priya grabbed her arm on one side, and Chelsea grabbed her arm on the other. They both squeezed hard, letting out little shrieks that the counsellors weren't supposed to hear.

"Oh, Gaby," whispered Priya, squeezing Gaby's hand so hard she thought it would fall off. "This is unbelievable!"

*Unbelievable is right,* Gaby thought. She'd never imagined when she'd first said Jake was her brother that there was *any* way she'd be sitting here in this position right now. Now she had to pretend she was leaving camp, going to Australia, and related to a semi-famous person. *Most people,* she thought to herself, *would not be able to pull this off.*

But Gaby had a plan.

# CHAPTER EIGHT

"This...is...huge." Priya's mouth was hanging open as they all stared at Gaby on the way back to the cabin. "I just can't believe it!" she continued in a whisper. "Your brother *totally* pulled it off. Your family is headed down under!"

Grace and Brynn trailed behind as everyone crowded around Gaby. Earlier, Grace had filled Brynn in on what had happened at campfire the night before, and just as Grace had suspected, Brynn *had* made her feel better.

"Grace, Chelsea and Priya have been crushing on Spence since camp started," Brynn had told her. "You can't take anything they say seriously. I'm sure they didn't mean to hurt your feelings. Of *course* you're crushworthy – and Spence would be nuts not to see that."

Grace had just smiled and said "thanks". What Priya and Chelsea had said still bothered her, but it was nice just to be reminded that *someone* in bunk 5A thought she was awesome.

Now Belle and Clarissa were in the mess hall, picking up the popcorn and hot chocolate that the girls would have to celebrate the end of *Survival Camp*. This meant that they were free to discuss Jake's win.

Gaby just looked shocked. "I still don't believe it," she said quietly. "I mean, I'm going to Australia. Tomorrow. It's all so crazy."

Grace frowned. "Don't you have to call your parents or something?"

Gaby turned to face her, startled. "Um...yeah!" She laughed nervously. "I guess I'm so in shock, I totally forgot that. You guys, I'm going to run back and call them from the payphone."

"It's weird they haven't tried to call you already, huh?" Tori asked. "It's been, like, an hour since he won."

Gaby looked stunned. Then she shrugged, looking more casual. "I'm sure they're in a complete frenzy," she said. "I'm sure they were on the phone with Jake, or the producers or something."

"Right," agreed Tori. "They probably had to be briefed by the lawyers."

Gaby beamed. "Right."

For a few seconds, nobody moved.

"All right," Brynn said, motioning with her hand. "Go ahead, Gaby! Aren't you dying to know the details?"

Gaby nodded quickly. "I am! Okay — see you in a few."

She took off, zigzagging across the sports field, back to the centre of camp. The rest of the girls turned to look at one another, smiling and shaking their heads.

"Wow," Natalie observed. "She's a mess."

"You would be too, if you were going to Australia tomorrow," Chelsea spoke up.

"I didn't mean anything snarky," Nat replied. "She just seems excited."

"I'm excited *for* her," Priya said.

"Yeah," Alex said slowly, "you guys seem close lately."

Priya shrugged. "We're all friends in 5A, aren't we?"

"Right," said Chelsea.

"We're all friends," echoed Candace.

*Right, we're all friends*, thought Grace, watching Priya and Chelsea. *Until you have the nerve to hang out with a boy someone else has a crush on, then watch out!*

"Do you think she'll have to leave camp tonight?" Jenna asked as they started walking towards the cabin again.

"Probably," Tori replied. "I mean, if they're leaving for Australia tomorrow. She'll need time to pack and everything."

Chelsea sighed. "It's too bad. I'll miss her."

Nat's eyes bugged out. "*You'll* miss *Gaby*?" she asked. Lately Chelsea and Gaby had been at each other's throats.

But Chelsea shrugged. "She's grown on me," she replied.

"Actually," Val spoke up, "she's kind of grown on me, too. These last couple of weeks — doesn't it seem like she's been a lot easier to deal with?"

Jenna nodded. "I never thought I'd say it, but yes. A lot less snarky."

Alyssa nodded. "And she's just been talking more."

By this time, they'd reached the cabin. Everyone piled in and wandered to their cubbies, grabbing their pyjamas. Grace moved in slow motion, not really interacting with anybody as she threw on her Scooby-Doo boxer shorts and a tank top. She shoved her curly red hair into a ponytail and took out her earrings.

Belle and Clarissa had arrived with the hot chocolate and popcorn, and by the time Gaby came back, everyone was sitting in a circle on the floor, chatting.

"Um, hey," Gaby said nervously, eyeing her counsellor.

"Hey," Belle replied in a curious voice. "Gaby, where were you?"

"I was at the payphone," Gaby said with a shrug. "Personal phone call."

"Was it an emergency?" Clarissa asked. "Because otherwise, you really should ask permission."

Gaby nodded. "Kind of."

"What's up?" Belle asked, looking concerned now. She put down her mug of hot chocolate and moved to stand up.

"Um," Gaby was saying. She looked across the room, a blank expression settling across her features, looking uncomfortable. "Mydogbrokehisfoot," she said finally, so fast you couldn't make out the words.

Grace caught Brynn's eye across the room. Their expressions were the same: *What the heck?* Why would Gaby still keep Jake's role in *Survival Camp* from their counsellors?

"What?" asked Clarissa.

"My dog broke his foot," Gaby replied, a little louder, seeming to come back to earth. "He's going to be fine, it turns out. But my parents mentioned it in their last e-mail and I got a little – worried."

"Oh," said Belle, looking surprised and a little relieved. She sat back down. "All right, good. But seriously, Gaby? Next time tell us where you're going."

Gaby nodded and smiled, moving in to join the circle. Everyone seemed to be struggling to catch her eye as she took a mug of hot chocolate and a bag of popcorn.

"*Survival Camp* was fun, wasn't it?" asked Clarissa as Gaby sat down on the floor. "I thought it might be kind of predictable, but it was full of surprises."

"You can say that again," murmured Grace, watching Gaby.

"No," Gaby whispered, carefully buttering an English muffin as she leaned in so all her friends could hear her. "They don't know yet. It's what the producers wanted."

Tori looked sceptical. "The producers told your parents to tell you to lie to the camp staff?" she asked. "Why? It's not like you can ruin the show. We all know how it ended."

Gaby shrugged. "Not just the staff. Turns out I wasn't supposed to tell you guys the truth, either. A lot of legal stuff I didn't understand," she replied. "This afternoon, my parents will come to pick me up and they'll explain everything to Dr. Steve then. For now, we pretend like everything is normal."

Tori's mouth sprang open to ask another question,

but right at that moment Clarissa came back, holding a fresh pitcher of orange juice. "All right, guys," she said. "Go easy on this one."

Grace sat back and thought as everyone started passing the pitcher around, and Belle, Keith and another counsellor stood up at the podium to make the morning announcements. There was definitely something weird going on with Gaby. Grace had had run-ins with Gaby before, dating back to her first summer, and she recognized the signs. But Grace didn't know what it was – she was probably just nervous about Australia, or trying to make the whole thing more dramatic to get even more attention. Whatever it was, Grace was sure it was dumb. And besides – she had her own problems to think about.

Problems like Spence. The social was that night, and Grace had stayed up practically all night wondering whether she should cancel their date. Could it be true that he was just a big flirt, and wasn't all that into her? She and Spence had fun together, sure. But what separated a just-friends vibe from a boyfriend vibe? Grace didn't know, and she knew that Priya had struggled with that question herself. Still, Grace had to admit that she *wanted* to go to the social with Spence. She wasn't even sure whether *she* was all that crazy about *him* – not in a romantic way, anyway. But she had a great time with him and she was definitely looking forward to it.

And then there was the Priya and Chelsea problem. So Priya and Chelsea still liked Spence. So what? Grace had trouble admitting it, but a big part of her felt *angry* at her friend Priya — angry that she could see a boy taking an interest in Grace and assume that he didn't really like her that much. Why should Grace sacrifice her happiness for them when they hadn't cared about her feelings?

She'd struggled with it for hours, but finally decided not to cancel the date. She really wanted to go. It would make her happy. When she'd mentioned it to Brynn before breakfast, she'd agreed 100 per cent — actually, she seemed stunned that Grace had even considered cancelling.

"What are you, nuts?" she'd asked. "Friend or *special* friend...the important thing is that if you go with Spence, then Jordan and I can double with you guys. It'll be the most fun double date the Camp Lakeview social has ever seen!"

"I'm going to miss you *so much*," Priya was saying as she hugged Gaby.

They were standing outside 5A's cabin. Inside,

Belle was still asleep, finishing up the siesta before dinner. Grace had offered to wake her up so Gaby could say goodbye, but Gaby had been weird about the whole thing – *oh, no, just let her sleep*. Clarissa was in the mess hall, setting the tables. It felt weird to be saying goodbye to Gaby without any counsellors around, but Gaby insisted her parents were in Dr. Steve's office, waiting.

"Have a *wonderful* time!" Brynn added. "We're going to miss you so much on the play."

"Oh!" Gaby jumped up like she'd forgotten about that. Her stunned expression soon turned to a calculating smile as she turned to Grace. "You know what? Grace, I give *you* the part of Sarah Brown." Grace's mouth dropped open.

"Um," Brynn replied. "I'm pretty sure you can't just *give* roles away like candy. Especially since the show is in two days. Plus, you have an understudy! Grace would probably have to audition against her."

Grace felt overwhelmed by the very idea. "You know, I just might let that one go."

Gaby shrugged. "All right. Just trying to be nice." She turned to the rest of the bunk and smiled. "Guys, I really have to get going! But thank you so much for the great send-off. I promise to write all about Australia on the blog, and I can't wait to see you at the reunion!"

Everyone rotated in to give Gaby one last hug. "Good luck," Grace said as she pulled away.

*Whatever you're up to*, she thought.

All the Gaby excitement made the girls ten minutes late waking up Belle (they told her Gaby was in Dr. Steve's office, but they didn't mention Jake or the show), which made them fifteen minutes late to dinner, which made Grace twenty minutes late getting to the newspaper room to help clean up from the découpage craft. All the third division to fifth division kids were going to go back to their bunks at seven o'clock to get ready for the dance, but they had a few minutes free between dinner and then. Spence and Grace had arranged to meet up in the newspaper room to tidy up a little. When Grace spotted Spence messily picking leaves and glue off the work table, she ran over.

"Sorry I'm late," she said, gathering the leaves into a neat pile and grabbing a trash can. "Um, let's try this way. You're going to get glue all over you."

"I am *not*," Spence replied with mock outrage, pushing his glasses up on his nose and sticking a leaf to his cheek in the process. "I'm doing great. Where were you, anyway? I saw your whole bunk come in late to dinner."

Grace sighed. "Yeah, we were late because we were saying goodbye to Gaby."

Spence looked surprised. "What?"

Grace nodded, grabbing a paper towel and some all-purpose cleaner out of the closet. "It was this whole big drama. But I guess I can tell you now, since Gaby's gone."

"She's gone?"

"Yeah." Grace removed the leaf from Spence's cheek and carefully tossed it in the trash. "You know the show we've been watching, *Survival Camp*?"

"Of course," Spence replied.

Grace nodded. "Well, the kid that won? Jake?"

"Yeah?"

"He's Gaby's brother." Grace sprayed the table with cleaner and realized that that just made the whole thing stickier. "Spence, I'm sorry. This is kind of turning into a mess."

"It was a mess before you got here." Spence grabbed a paper towel from her. He sprayed some more cleaner and started scrubbing, and to Grace's surprise, the glue came up. "Wait a minute, what? Grace is related to the guy who won? And she left?"

Grace nodded. "He's her brother," she said.

"*Seriously*? So why did she leave?"

Grace shrugged. "Why do you *think*? She's going with her family to Australia."

119

Spence just looked at Grace for a moment, not saying anything. Grace figured he must be surprised – her whole bunk had been *plenty* surprised when Gaby first gave them the news.

"Grace," Spence said finally, quietly. "When did Gaby leave?"

"Right before dinner," Grace said. "That's why we were late."

Spence frowned. "There's no way."

"What do you mean?"

Spence sighed. "In the morning, I take nature, right?" he said, his voice still quiet. "I guess our counsellor got inspired by Dr. Steve letting us watch *Survival Camp*, because this morning she wheeled this big TV into our meeting so we could watch this piece on *The Today Show* about a scientist who discovered a new bug."

Grace furrowed her eyebrows. "Um, that's great," she replied. "But what does that have to do with Gaby?"

"Right before the bug story, there was this piece about that kid, Jake, and his family," Spence went on. "First of all, he had a sister and brother with him – both little kids. And second of all, they were leaving for the airport *right after* the interview."

Grace frowned, trying to take this all in.

"Wow. So Gaby *lied* about being Jake's sister!"

Which meant...

"I guess she can't be going to Australia," she said.

Which meant...

"Oh no," Grace murmured. "Gaby's not with her parents. So where *is* she?"

# CHAPTER NINE

Gaby's bag was *enormous*. She'd stashed a bunch of her things in the laundry building, figuring she could have the camp send them later, and had only taken the "essentials". But now she could see that even the "essentials" were way too heavy to carry. She let her duffel bag fall to the ground for the tenth time and paused to rest on a log.

She pulled the hiking map of Camp Lakeview's property out of her pocket to check her progress. She was taking the Elm Trail, a "moderate" trail that locals used for cross-country skiing in the winter. But Gaby didn't care about any of that. What she cared about was that it crossed a main road about three kilometres away from the centre of camp – route 17. Once Gaby reached that road, she could flag down a ride, get to the bus station, and hopefully be home in Philadelphia before nightfall.

Gaby sighed, wishing she had thought to bring a bottle of water or some snacks. She was missing dinner, and the fact that her bag unexpectedly weighed twenty tons was slowing her down, meaning that it would probably be hours before she ate. For the first time, Gaby felt a twinge of nervousness – or maybe it was just hunger – in her belly. *I kind of thought I'd have reached the road by now.*

Slowly, Gaby stood up. She grabbed her bag – every time she put it down it seemed to get heavier – and heaved it over her shoulder. She shoved the map back in her pocket and started walking at a good clip. *I just have to keep moving, and eventually I'll hit it.*

She had to leave camp. That was the downside of this whole Jake debacle. But given the situation, it wasn't like she really had a choice. Could she go back to her friends and admit that she had lied about the whole thing? *Uh, no.* So leaving was the only option. And she'd miss everybody, but a little part of her was really eager to get back to air conditioning, her personal broadband connection and her digital cable. She'd been living in the wilderness a little too long.

Of course she'd have to come up with a story to tell her parents. They'd be surprised to see her. But Gaby had all that figured out. She'd tell them that camp was terrible this year, that Chelsea was being horrible and mean, and that she just couldn't take it any more. Her parents would understand – they always took her side. They'd call Dr. Steve – Gaby would make them promise not to mention Chelsea – and *ta-da!* Gaby would get to stay home and bunk 5A would still think she was in Australia.

*It's the perfect plan.* Gaby smiled to herself, still thrilled that she'd thought it all up. Of course, she knew it was *possible* that people would figure out she'd left without permission, and that there was a *slight* chance they'd catch her before she worked it all out. Then she'd just tell Dr. Steve that she was having a horrible time in camp, not getting along with anyone, and be vague about the specifics so as not to single out any one culprit.

*CRACK!*

Gaby jumped, wondering what she might have broken inside her bag. The glasses that she was supposed to wear to read? The retainer she was supposed to wear to bed? She took a deep breath, calming herself down. *No big deal. Whatever it is, it's nothing Mom and Dad can't replace.*

She pulled out the map she'd stolen from Belle's binder last night while everyone was asleep. Belle had written in little sketches of landmarks for bunk hikes. There were two little wavy lines that crossed Elm trail about halfway to the road. *A brook?* Gaby wondered.

*Some vines? Snakes?* Gaby's skin crawled. While she was willing to do what she had to do to get home, she wasn't exactly a huge fan of the outdoors.

*If that's a brook,* Gaby thought, *I can't believe I haven't passed it by now.* According to her watch, it had been a full hour since she'd left her friends and snuck into the woods. *An hour to go maybe a kilometre and a half?* Gaby shook her head. She knew she was no champion hiker, but *come on.*

Standing up and stretching before she grabbed her duffel bag again, Gaby's eye caught on a pine tree. The trunk had broken about three metres from the ground, and the pointed top was still attached, bent down over the ground at a 45-degree angle. The tree looked like a sideways seven. But more importantly, it reminded Gaby of one of Belle's little chicken-scratch illustrations. She unfolded the map again and scanned the line for Elm Trail.

Sure enough, the broken tree was sketched in – not even halfway to the little brook/vines/snakes.

Gaby's heart began to pound. It was the middle of the summer, but the sun was already starting to go down. It was getting late. She couldn't believe she'd only gotten less than a kilometre. But then, she'd been dragging the stupid bag and taking lots of breaks. Plus, the terrain wasn't terrible, but it wasn't easy either – the path was littered with rocks, plants and tree roots.

Gaby clutched the shoulder strap of her bag. Could she leave it? Or could she take out some of the stuff she didn't need? Her heart pounded even faster as she realized *no, I can't.* She'd never have the chance to come back and get that stuff. And all the "essentials" really were *essential.* What would she leave? Her Juicy Couture hoodie? Her Abercrombie bikini? The fancy stationery her parents had packed for her, engraved with her full name and address? *I don't think so.*

*Which means that I just have to deal with it.* With another big sigh, she hoisted the bag onto her shoulder. *It's all right,* she told herself. *It won't be easy. But it'll all be worth it when I'm sitting at home eating Ben & Jerry's.*

Gaby started walking again. She got a queasy feeling when she noticed how dark the woods looked now.

*Just keep walking,* Gaby told herself. *You'll make it.*

Gaby couldn't take it any more. She had to sit down and try to adjust her sneakers. She could feel the blisters coming on, and she had no idea how long she'd been hiking. She'd never noticed the brook or snakes or whatever Belle had been referring to. To be honest, she wasn't even sure she was on the right path any more.

Gaby actually heard a creaking sound as she threw her bag to the ground and stood up straight to stretch.

*I'm like an old person*, Gaby thought to herself. *Like Dr. Steve.* But then, the hike so far had been miserable, and her bag felt like six elephants strapped to her back. With a moan, Gabby collapsed onto the ground. She sat up Indian-style and carefully pulled off her shoes and socks. Four blisters. Two on each foot. She closed her eyes and tried to calm her breathing. *How am I ever going to make it to the road?*

She felt sore all over. And it had grown so dark, she was having trouble seeing more than three metres in front of her. Soon it would be completely dark – and then what would she do?

Gaby took a few deep breaths, but they came out shaky. *I will not cry. I will not cry.* She willed herself to put her shoes back on and stand, ignoring her painful blisters and cursing herself for not bringing Band-Aids. It occurred to her that, for the first time, she missed some of her bunkmates. Actually, she would love the company of Priya, or Alex, or even Grace or Chelsea right now. *What if I have to sleep out here by myself?* Gaby shuddered. She didn't even want to think about it.

She grabbed her bag and walked on. She didn't know where she was going, or what she would do if she ended up on the wrong trail. The only thing that mattered was getting away from camp and making sure her friends never found out she'd lied.

Just as the last bit of light faded, Gaby came upon a little clearing. A couple of rocks sat in a grassy area, surrounded by a little circle of trees. Up ahead, the path wound through a break in the woods. She followed it without thinking. When she got a couple of metres from the trees, she gasped.

*The road.*

She'd finally reached it!

Relief flooded through her like a cool drink on a hot day. She dumped her bag on the side of the road and quickly ran her fingers through her hair, hoping she didn't look like too much of a hobbit. She brushed dirt and leaves off her tank and capris, and sat down on her bag to wait for a car to pass.

Gaby knew hitchhiking was dangerous, but who was going to hurt her in the middle of nowhere? After she'd been sitting only a minute, she heard a car approaching. Soon the car appeared over the hill. She stood up, pasted on her sweetest smile, and stuck out her thumb.

The car didn't even slow down before passing her by.

Gaby was stunned. Didn't she look adorable and helpless? It was almost completely dark now. She couldn't even read her watch to tell what time it was, but it had to be three or four hours since she left camp.

Five more minutes passed without a car.

Then ten.

Gaby shivered, grabbed her hoodie out of her bag, and wrapped it around her. The road was totally dark and silent, except for a hooting in the distance. Gaby didn't know any more whether she was shivering from the cold or from the creepy feeling that descended over her.

*What if no one picks me up?*

# CHAPTER TEN

"Tell me again what happened, from the beginning," Dr. Steve said, looking them all over with a grave expression. All of bunk 5A was collected in his office, including Belle and Clarissa.

Grace took a deep breath. Since she'd gone to Dr. Steve in the first place, she'd been more or less elected spokesperson for the whole bunk. "After the first episode, Gaby told us that Jake was her brother. And right after he won, she said she was going to go to Australia with her family. That night, she took off and said she was going to call her parents from a payphone."

Dr. Steve cast a stern look in Belle's direction. "And you didn't know about this?"

Belle shook her head, still looking stunned. "I was getting the hot chocolate and popcorn with Clarissa," she replied. "I noticed she was gone, but when she came back she said something about an emergency.

That she heard her dog broke his foot and wanted to talk to her parents about it."

Dr. Steve turned his stern expression on all the campers. "None of you thought it was odd that Gaby would lie to Belle?"

"I did," Grace admitted. "But Gaby lies about little stuff all the time. I thought she was up to something, but I *never* thought she would have made up the whole thing, or that she'd run away from camp."

Dr. Steve looked back at Belle. "And you never heard any of this? Gaby never shared with you that she had a brother on *Survival Camp*?"

Belle shook her head. "None of the girls told me." She glanced sadly at her campers, none of whom would meet her eye. "She probably thought I would ask too many questions, or catch on that she was lying. I'm sure it wasn't an accident that she didn't tell any of the camp staff."

"She told us not to tell anyone," Natalie spoke up. "She said she'd get in trouble with the producers if they knew she'd told."

"And we *never* thought Jake would win," Jenna added. "No offence. I know you guys were really into him. But we all thought he'd be voted out, even Gaby."

"Besides," Brynn murmured from her spot next to Grace, "we had no reason to think Gaby would lie."

Dr. Steve sighed deeply. "No reason," he repeated. "Girls, do you remember the talk we had when you first got to camp?"

All the campers visibly wilted. Grace didn't react much, though — she still didn't know exactly what had been said.

Clarissa spoke up. "I remember. And I'm sure all the girls do, too."

"The weird thing is," Belle added sadly, "they've been doing so much better these two weeks. Everyone gets along, and there haven't been any fights that I've seen."

Alex looked confused. "Can I ask a question?" she asked.

Dr. Steve nodded. "You may."

Alex scrunched up her eyebrows. "What does us being cliquey, or not being cliquey, have to do with Gaby lying about being related to Jake?"

Dr. Steve frowned and leaned back in his chair, tenting his fingers. "What does one have to do with the other?" he asked. "Let me turn that question back on you. Girls, do any of you have any idea?"

Grace glanced over at her friends. The girls who used to feel like her best friends in the world, but lately had made her feel left out — not even on purpose, but just by talking about things she hadn't been there to experience, and not explaining things fully. Even Brynn, her best best friend, had seemed a little distant lately – distracted by her work on the play. They all looked totally confused, even annoyed that Dr. Steve seemed to think there could be a connection. Alex just sat there, shaking her head. Priya caught Chelsea's eye and rolled her eyes when Dr. Steve wasn't looking.

"I think I might know," Grace said quietly.

"Yes, Grace," Dr. Steve said gently. "Please tell us your theory."

"I think..." Grace paused, uncomfortable with all the attention. She knew her friends, especially Brynn, had to be wondering what the heck she was doing. Agreeing with Dr. Steve and going against her girls? She had to be crazy. And besides Priya and Chelsea, it wasn't like Grace had a real beef with any of her bunkmates. They hadn't been outwardly mean, or tried to exclude her from any conversations. They just...hadn't included her.

"I think Gaby might have lied so she'd feel like she fitted in," Grace finished. "Maybe she felt like not enough people were paying attention to her, or maybe she felt like she was getting the wrong kind of attention. Maybe she just wanted somebody to talk to her and take an interest. You know."

Dr. Steve nodded slowly. "I think that's very smart, Grace."

He looked back over the cluster of campers. Grace tried to fold into herself, not meeting anyone's eyes. She hadn't meant to speak up, but she knew what Dr. Steve was talking about.

Still looking a little confused, Brynn reached over and gave Grace's arm a supportive squeeze. Grace shot her a grateful look. *We'll talk later,* Brynn mouthed.

"So here we are," Dr. Steve continued. "We have a very close, but sometimes cliquey, group of girls. And we have one young girl out wandering the area, who knows where, doing who knows what. How do we solve this problem?"

"We have to find her," Priya spoke up.

"Right." Dr. Steve sat forward in his chair and looked at them sternly. "Tonight is the night of the social. But I'm afraid that none of you will be attending. Instead, you're going to be forming groups — with Clarissa, Belle and I as your leaders — and combing the area to look for Gaby. I know this must be a familiar scenario, after what you went through last session. How do you feel about that?"

The girls squirmed and avoided one another's eyes. Nobody was happy about it, but they all knew Gaby had to be found.

"In the meantime," Dr. Steve continued, "I would like you all to wait outside while I call Gaby's parents.

They have a right to know she left camp. When I'm finished, we'll split up the teams and head out to look for her."

Everyone nodded, slowly shaking off their surprise and getting up. Grace spotted many of the girls giving her funny looks as they wandered out, but she didn't react. She was only worried about one thing right now: finding Gaby. As impulsive and hot-headed as Gaby was, who *knew* what kind of trouble she might be getting into?

"All right," Belle announced, flicking her flashlight on and pointing it at the trail ahead of her. "My trail map, the map that shows all the hiking trails on Camp Lakeview land, was ripped out of my binder. We're *assuming* Gaby had something to do with that. So we're all going to split up and search different areas."

Brynn raised her hand, looking shell-shocked and nervous. The seriousness of Gaby's disappearance seemed to have hit all the girls by now, and there were no smiles, no chatter — everyone stood stiffly in their pre-assigned groups, waiting to leave.

"Yes, Brynn?" Dr. Steve asked.

"Um, it's pretty late," Brynn said quietly. "It's been hours since she left. What if she's not on camp property any more? What if she's, I don't know —" her voice cracked a little — "wandering the town?"

Dr. Steve nodded and touched Brynn's shoulder. "We're aware of the hour, Brynn, and the local police have been contacted. Their patrol cars will be looking for anyone who meets Gaby's description. They've been very cooperative and have promised to look for her." He paused. "But if Gaby doesn't want to be found, it's possible that she's hiding in the woods, or camping. It's up to us to search as much as we can and make sure she's not right under our noses."

Grace glanced over at her teammates, Priya and Chelsea. The three of them would be searching with Belle. Priya blinked like she was trying to hold back tears. Grace's heart was beating fast. She couldn't wait to start looking so they could find Gaby and get her safely back to camp.

"Guys," Belle said, walking over with a copy of the trail map, "we're going to be searching the Elm, Hemlock and Sassafras trails. They all cross over one another, but we're still going to have to make pretty good time if we want to search them all before nine. So let's get moving."

Grace sighed. They had less than two hours. At nine o'clock, Gaby's parents were set to arrive and the matter would be officially turned over to the police.

With listless waves to their bunkmates, Grace, Priya and Chelsea followed Belle into the woods.

Priya looked miserable. "This is awful. We're missing the social, and Gaby might be lost, or hurt. We should have told you sooner that she was going to leave, Belle."

"Yeah," Chelsea agreed. "We just assumed you knew."

Belle frowned. "Well, I didn't," she replied.

Grace felt her face flush. "I'm sorry," she said. "We should have told you. Are you going to get in trouble?"

"Let's not worry about that right now." Belle stopped and pulled out the map. "Well, at least we're on the right path. There's that broken pine tree." She gestured to a tree that had broken and folded over on itself, like a sideways number seven. Grace shivered, but she wasn't sure whether it was from the cool air or her own nervousness. Where was Gaby? Where could she be at this hour of the night where she was safe, and where someone wouldn't have contacted the camp? Grace didn't want to think about it.

Suddenly she felt a hand on her shoulder and turned to see Priya, looking sympathetic. "Grace," Priya said softly, "I'm sorry you're missing the social. I know Spence was looking forward to going with you."

Grace was surprised. First of all, that she hadn't even thought about the dance, or Spence, until that point.

And second of all...*Priya* thought Spence was really looking forward to going with Grace? Priya, who'd told her not to get her hopes up since Spence was such a big flirt? Grace didn't know what to say.

"Yeah," she said finally. "I mean, maybe. I dunno. The truth is..." She sighed. "I'm much more worried about just finding Gaby."

"Me too," agreed Priya.

"Me three," added Chelsea, slipping up next to Priya. "Listen, Grace, I think it was really great that you and Spence figured out that Gaby lied. We might never have figured it out, and who knows what would have happened to Gaby?"

"Thanks," said Grace. "I mean, it was Spence that had the info. And it's no big deal – you guys would have figured it out and told Dr. Steve, too."

"I guess," agreed Priya. "Listen, Grace..." She stopped, like she wasn't sure what to say next.

"What?" asked Grace. "Listen, whatever it is, Priya, you don't have to worry about it right now."

"No, I want to say this." Priya glanced over at Chelsea. "I think Chelsea feels this, too. I'm really sorry if I made you feel..." She trailed off.

"Unlikable?" Grace asked.

"Right." Priya glanced down, looking sheepish. "I mean, I really wasn't trying to hurt you, and I thought I was just being honest. But when I think about it, I have to admit that I still have a little crush on Spence..."

"And so do I," Chelsea admitted.

"And I guess maybe — that might have influenced what I thought about you guys." Priya looked into the woods, still avoiding Grace's eyes.

Grace looked at her friend. "It's cool, Priya," she said finally. "I mean, I know you wouldn't say anything mean about me. And you know what? I'm not totally sure I like him like a boyfriend or whatever. But if I do? I think that should be okay. Even if you guys liked him, or like him."

Priya sighed and closed her eyes. "I know. You're right."

Chelsea looked upset, but when Priya opened her eyes and gave her a *look*, she softened. "All right. If he *does* like you...I guess it's not your fault."

"Right," Grace replied.

Suddenly Priya jumped up and wrapped her arms around Grace in a huge hug. "I'm sorry!" she said. "I'm glad we figured this all out. I don't want to ever stop being your friend, Grace."

"Me too!" cried Chelsea, piling on top in a group hug.

"Uh, great," Grace replied, struggling to breathe. "Guys? Let's save this for after we find Gaby."

"Right!" Chelsea and Priya said at once, pulling away.

"And hey," said Priya, falling into step behind Grace as they continued after Belle. "Let's never let boys come between us again."

"Right," agreed Chelsea, smiling.

"Right," said Grace.

But she had a feeling it was going to be harder in practice.

"Guys," Belle said with a sigh, "we've got half an hour to go. We really, really should head back."

Grace's heart sank. They'd been hiking for over an hour now, and so far, no signs of Gaby. It had been too dark to completely search the trail, but still — Grace had thought they'd find footprints, or a hairband, or *something* to prove that Gaby had been there. She couldn't explain it, she just had this strong *feeling* that Gaby had come this way, disappearing into the hiking trails.

"Five more minutes," Grace begged.

"Fine," Belle replied. "But I really don't think she came this way. And even if we go back, it's not a total loss — maybe one of the other search teams found something."

Grace didn't reply. She was scouring the ground and the trees, using her flashlight to search every square centimetre of surface. Then suddenly, she heard a sound. It was a familiar sound, like a sigh — like all the trees suddenly breathing out at once.

A *car!*

"Guys," Grace said, "do you hear that?"

Priya scrunched up her eyebrows in concentration. "That?" she said finally. "Is that a car?"

"Probably," Belle replied, looking at the map. "This trail crosses route 17 right through those trees."

*Route 17.* Grace felt her pulse quickening. "Belle," she said, "do you think Gaby might have gone to a main road? Maybe she'd try to hitchhike?"

Belle looked horrified. "Hitchhiking is so dangerous!" she cried. "I'd hope Gaby would know that."

Priya shook her head. "Gaby may know that in her head. But when she really sets her mind to something..."

Belle looked thoughtful. She shone her flashlight through the break in the trees, then started walking. "Come on, guys," she called behind her. "Let's check it out."

Priya, Chelsea and Grace followed closely behind. Route 17 was deserted at this time of night. Camp Lakeview was located in a tiny town to begin with, and it seemed like they rolled up the sidewalks at 8 p.m. It was completely dark now, and Grace got a creepy chill from all the silence. She looked up and down the street. Gaby was nowhere to be seen.

"Huh," said Belle, sweeping the beam of her flashlight back and forth. "Well, I guess we should be relieved. Maybe Gaby's smart enough not to hitchhike after all."

But Priya was aiming her flashlight at the ground. "Belle," she said suddenly, urgency in her voice.

They all followed the beam of Priya's light to the ground. A pink flowered luggage tag lay in the grass.

GABY PARSONS. PHILADELPHIA, PA .

# CHAPTER ELEVEN

"You are *so* right," Gaby was saying, grabbing the armrest between the truck's seats as it sped around a curve. "Paris Hilton *is* underrated."

Her host glanced at her with an approving smile, then snapped her gum and ran a finger through her unruly, ruby-dyed hair. "I'm not saying she's the next Britney," she said cheerfully, taking another curve on two wheels. "But it must be hard to be taken seriously when you're, you know, a socialite."

Gaby just nodded.

The girl slammed on the brake to stop at a red light and both she and Gaby lurched forwards. "So, you wanted to go to...?"

"The *bus station*." Gaby spoke as loudly and clearly as possible. She had the sense she wasn't dealing with a rocket scientist here. But whatever. This girl might be a few tacos short of a combo platter, but she had a driver's licence, and that's all Gaby cared about.

"The bus station. Riiiight." The light turned, and the girl punched the gas. They careened through the intersection, missing the turn that would take them to the centre of town. "Mind if we make a quick stop first? I just remembered, I left my licence back at my apartment."

*Greeeeaaaaat*, thought Gaby. *If we get pulled over, which is likely, since this girl never slows down, they'll find an under-age fugitive riding with an unlicensed speed demon. Perfect!* But she said, "Sure, that's fine." The sooner they got this girl's licence, the sooner they could get to the bus station and Gaby could be on her way home.

"What did you say your name was again?" the girl asked as they drove back into a wooded area.

"Gaby," Gaby replied calmly. "Gaby Jolie? I'm a college student."

"Riiiight," the girl replied. "I'm Charisma." Charisma blew a huge bubble with her gum. "So you were camping with your friends?"

"Yeah, and we got separated," Gaby agreed. It was the story she'd come up with last night. "My one friend probably thinks I'm still with my boyfriend, and my boyfriend probably thinks I'm with my friend. You know how it is."

"Sure," the girl replied. "Like, right now? My cat

probably thinks I'm out with my pet turtle."

Gaby gripped the armrest a little harder. "Riiiight."

Charisma took one hand off the wheel to pull the gum off her face, then swerved to avoid hitting something in the road. "Did you see that?! It looked like a panther!"

"I think it was a squirrel," Gaby replied, starting to wonder if she was going to make it to the bus station. *It's a good thing this is a one-horse town,* she thought to herself. *There aren't many people or cars for her to slam into.* "Um, where's your apartment?"

"Right up here." Sounding calmer, Charisma pulled off onto a dirt road. Gaby relaxed as they drove through some trees and past a few small shedlike buildings. *Last stop,* she thought, *and then it's the bus station and home for me.* She felt a little giddy at the thought of being so close to finished. *I really pulled this off!*

A cluster of buildings came into focus up ahead. Gaby smiled, relieved to have survived the ride to Charisma's apartment, but just as quickly, the bottom dropped out of her stomach. In the middle of the log-cabin buildings was a flagpole – flying the *Camp Lakeview* flag! And suddenly, Gaby realized she was looking at the mess hall, the gym and the camp offices – all from the rear.

"Hey!" Gaby cried. "What the—"

"Here's the deal," Charisma announced in a totally different, less ditzy voice, parking the car and turning in her seat to face Gaby. "I'm a Camp Lakeview legacy. I live around here now, and I know that college students don't often turn up on deserted roads dragging duffel bags and looking *maybe* thirteen."

Gaby pouted, stung. "Try *fourteen*."

"Whatever." The girl waved her arm like, *who cares?* "I don't know what the heck you were thinking, even *considering* getting into a car with a stranger. I could be anybody! I could be a serial killer!"

Gaby scowled. "But you're not."

"Because you're *lucky!*" Charisma glowered. "Now, we're going in there and I'm handing you over to the camp president. I don't know what little squabble you had with your bunkmates, but you're going to have to work it out or call your parents. And don't even *think* about pulling a fast one on me. I play dumb well — especially when I need to distract someone from where we're headed — but I am *not* really dumb," she said, getting out of the truck and around the back to get Gaby's bag.

For a moment, Gaby considered making a run for it. Sure, she'd have to lose the bag. But maybe she could make it to the bus station on foot? She shuddered, realizing that her bunkmates were probably at the social right now, thinking she was on a plane to Australia. What would she tell them?

"Gabrielle?"

Gaby was stunned by her mother's voice. She looked up and spotted her mom running towards the truck from across the parking lot, where her own car was parked. Gaby's dad stood outside the driver's-side door, a mixture of confusion and relief on his face.

Gaby opened the door and ran to her mom without thinking. "Mom!" Before she could remember what she'd been about to do, she was pressed up against her mother's chest, crying.

Dr. Steve looked at Gaby warily from behind his desk. "What you've done, Gaby, is grounds for expulsion," he said.

*Expulsion. Yes! Just like I planned.* Gaby rubbed her nose and tried to look crushed. "I know," she said quietly. "I really messed up."

"You really did," Dr. Steve agreed. "Do you have any idea how much danger you put yourself in? You might have been injured on the trails, and who would have helped you alone at night? You were extremely foolish to hitchhike. As Charisma told you, she might have been anyone. I shudder to think what kind of character might pick up a young girl in the middle of the woods."

Gaby shuddered. Actually, she hadn't thought of it that way. A few more tears leaked from her eyes.

Dr. Steve handed Gaby a tissue and then sat back in his chair, rubbing his chin. "Tell me again why you ran away, Gaby."

"It was everyone!" Gaby cried, sticking to her script. She was impressed by how genuine she sounded, now that her voice was raspy from crying. She took the tissue and blew her nose, turning to her father with the puppy-dog eyes. "I know I really shouldn't have left, and now I've wasted a lot of your money since I'm going to be expelled. But everyone was *so* mean to me this summer!"

Dr. Steve looked sceptical, but Gaby could see that her mother was struggling with whether or not to believe her.

Dr. Steve reached out, took the crumpled-up tissue, and threw it into the trash behind him. "Here's the thing, Gaby," he said. "I talked to all of your bunkmates. And your story doesn't match up with theirs."

Gaby's mouth dropped open. He talked to her *bunkmates?* She hadn't been expecting that. *Thank goodness I'll be expelled and won't have to face them.* She felt fresh tears coming on as she fished for a way to save this. "That's because they *hate* me! They don't want to get in trouble and they're all against me!"

Dr. Steve held up his hand as if to say, "Enough." A few hot tears leaked out of Gaby's eyes. "They all agree," he went on, "that *you* told *them* you had an older brother." He glanced up at Gaby's parents. "A boy by the name of Jake."

Gaby's dad's brow creased in confusion. "Gabrielle is an only child," he insisted.

"Exactly," replied Dr. Steve. "And Jake is a contestant on a reality programme that we watched. *Survival Camp.* The only problem is, he ended up winning the competition, and Gaby had to leave camp to make it look like she was on the prize vacation with his family."

Gaby felt her heart thumping hard. She could feel her parents looking at her, surprised and disappointed, but she couldn't look back at them. This certainly wasn't the first time she'd lied to them, but it was the first time she'd been caught in a lie this big and it frightened her.

"Why would you do that, Gaby?" her mom asked, sounding concerned. "Why would you make up such a preposterous story?"

Gaby didn't answer for a second.

"It was them!" she said finally, desperately. "They were all excluding me, and I—"

"Again," Dr. Steve broke in, looking sternly at Gaby, "that doesn't match up with your bunkmates' stories."

Gaby looked at the floor. Her face felt hot, and she had a lump in her throat.

She didn't say anything.

After a moment, Dr. Steve sighed and shifted in his seat. "Gaby's bunkmates," he went on, "seem to think that Gaby sometimes has trouble relating to the rest of them. She can be bossy or she can be overly sharp. They all agree that the Gaby–Chelsea dynamic isn't a good one, but they say Gaby came up with this lie on her own." He paused. "Possibly as a bid for some positive attention."

Gaby felt her mother's hand on her arm.

"I don't understand," Gaby's father said. "Gaby's a great kid. At home, she's very popular."

Gaby's mother rubbed her arm. Her voice was gentle, but insistent. "Gaby *says* she's very popular," she corrected. "But sometimes, she seems lonely."

Gaby kept staring at the floor. Tears welled up again, and one slid down her nose and plopped on the ground. Actually, Gaby was lonely a lot. She had a couple of close friends, but they were best friends with each other, not her. And lots of the time, Gaby felt left out – like she had to compete for their attention.

At camp, she liked feeling like she was surrounded

by friends. Until she slipped and said something snarky, and then she was alone again.

Her mom moved her hand to Gaby's back and began rubbing, then pulled Gaby close.

"Maybe," her mom was saying, "Gaby feels awkward making new friends."

Gaby started to cry then. It wasn't like when she'd been crying before, when she'd just been so relieved to see her mom and that she wasn't alone any more that the waterworks had turned on. Now she was sobbing big, heavy sobs.

Dr. Steve watched them all. "Listen," he said. "As I explained, this would normally be grounds for expulsion."

Even through her sobs, Gaby stiffened. *Normally? I have to go home!*

"But in Gaby's case," Dr. Steve went on, "I think it would be a greater punishment, and a greater lesson, for her to *stay* at camp. To face the friends she's lied to. And to try to find some healthier ways to make friends."

Gaby felt like her stomach had dropped out. Her sobs reached a fever pitch and her mother rubbed her back.

"I think you're right, Dr. Steve," her father agreed. He looked at Gaby. "Gaby, I'm sorry you feel left out, but I think you must learn a lesson from this behaviour.

And I can tell you that after camp, your punishment won't be over. You're going to spend a few weeks grounded and doing extra chores, so you'll have plenty of time to think about how foolish this was."

Gaby shook with sobs. She couldn't believe this. *I can't believe I have to face my whole bunk again. How did I screw this up so badly?*

Dr. Steve handed her another tissue. "You know, Gaby, there are easier ways to make friends."

Gaby nodded, trying to pull herself together. She wiped her eyes again, trying to halt her sobs. "I don't know what they are, though."

She looked up at Dr. Steve, and he met her eyes. "Maybe it's time to learn."

# CHAPTER TWELVE

"Hey," Priya said, falling into step beside Grace and touching her arm. "Don't beat yourself up. We searched as hard as we could."

"Yeah," Chelsea added, coming up on Priya's other side. "And you were the best one of the four of us."

Grace just shook her head. "I didn't find her, though," she said sadly. "In the end, that's what matters."

"Come on, Grace," Priya said gently. "If it wasn't for you, we never would have checked the road and found the luggage tag."

"Yeah," added Chelsea. "Now even if another team *hasn't* found her, we can tell the police where she was, and where she probably caught a ride."

Grace just sighed and nodded.

By this time, they'd walked back onto the main camp grounds. Loud music floated over from the gym, where a dull roar of voices and flashing coloured lights reminded them of the social they were missing.

"Spence must be lonely," Chelsea said with a teasing smile as they passed by the gym.

"You know what's funny?" Grace asked, realizing as she said it. "I haven't thought of him once since we've been out here. What happened to Gaby just seems more important now."

Priya nodded slowly. "Right."

The lights were on in bunk 5A's cabin, and they could hear voices inside, low and serious. Grace had butterflies in her stomach. *Oh no. They didn't find her, either. They're probably in there with the police!*

With a deep sigh, Belle swung the door open and gestured for them to enter. "Home again, home again, ladies."

With a heavy heart, Grace followed Priya and Chelsea in. In the main room, all the rest of 5A were sitting in a semicircle. Grace felt her stomach drop. Until she noticed who was sitting in the middle.

*Gaby!*

Gaby's eyes and nose were bright red, like she'd been crying for a while. It wasn't until Grace had digested the idea that Gaby had been found that she noticed Dr.

Steve sitting next to her. Gaby's eyes were downcast and she looked exhausted, nothing like her usual alert self. "Anyway," she was saying. "I know it was wrong and I'm so, *so* sorry for making you guys worry."

"Gaby!" Priya cried out and rushed towards her friend, throwing her arms around Gaby. "Oh, I'm *so* glad you're safe! We found your luggage tag by the road and we got *so* worried."

Gaby looked up at Priya, her dark eyes surprised and grateful. "Thanks, Priya," she said softly. In the same quiet voice, she told them all about her adventures: stupidly sticking her thumb out for a ride to the bus station, only to get picked up by Charisma.

"No! *Way!*" Natalie cried as the rest of the bunk started cracking up. "She did *not*! Say! That Paris! Hilton! Is *underrated!*"

Gaby managed a little smile. "She did," she said sheepishly. "And later? She thought a squirrel was a panther. And she was driving like a crazy person, and she told me she didn't even have her *licence.*" She shook her head. "I thought, if the cops pull us over, we're a fugitive and a mentally ill person without a licence. We're so dead."

The rest of the bunk erupted in giggles. Even Grace had to laugh at that one. Gaby's smile grew a little and she looked away, a pleased expression on her face.

"It turns out Charisma was kidding, though," she continued. "She needed an excuse not to go to the bus station right away, and she was acting dumb to keep me from noticing that we were driving right back to camp. I was really mad at her for taking me back here, but all things considered, it was pretty nice of her."

"*Very* nice of her," agreed Dr. Steve.

"Very nice of her," Gaby echoed with a smile.

"Well," Dr. Steve said, standing up and looking at Belle, "I think Gaby is back in capable hands. We've had a long talk, and Gaby is going to be helping out in the mess hall instead of taking electives next session." He paused. "She's also going to be e-mailing her parents every day, and helping out in my office each morning before breakfast. So I can keep an eye on her." He smiled gently at Gaby.

To Grace's surprise, Gaby smiled back, sheepishly.

"And she will not be allowed to perform in the play this weekend. Her role will be played by her understudy." Gaby looked disappointed by that part of her punishment, but she seemed to understand. *How funny,* Grace thought, *that the role I was so jealous of barely seems to matter at all any more.* Actually, she was looking forward to watching the play – from the audience.

Dr. Steve looked at his watch. "It's nine thirty," he announced. "I know I said earlier that bunk 5A would not be attending the social, but since you all worked so hard to find Gaby, I'll tell you what. You can all head over to the gym for the final hour."

Everyone jumped up, cheering and whooping.

"All *right!*" Brynn cheered. "Jordan will be so surprised to see me!"

Everyone stood up, and as Dr. Steve left, Tori announced, "No hair and make-up, ladies. There's no time. Let's get our *au naturel* butts over to the gym."

Everyone slowly moved towards the door, pausing to give Gaby a hug or an affectionate squeeze of the shoulder.

"I can't believe you thought you needed to go to all that trouble just to be our friend," said Priya.

"It's true," said Brynn. "When you think about it, we're not even that great."

"Though it is interesting that you're more comfortable trudging through the dark forest than just being plain ol' friendly," Natalie said as she gave Gaby a wink.

"I'm glad you're back," Alex told her, "even if you are a pain sometimes."

Behind her, Jenna grinned and punched Gaby's shoulder. "It wouldn't have been the same without you, that's for sure."

\* \* \*

"So what was that about?" Brynn asked softly as she and Grace walked to the gym together. They'd fallen a little behind their bunkmates, and Brynn watched Grace with a concerned expression.

"What do you mean?" Grace asked.

"What you told Dr. Steve." Brynn furrowed her eyebrows. "Do you really feel left out, Grace? I was thinking about it, and I realized that yeah, we probably talk a lot about stuff you missed." She looked sheepish.

Grace shrugged. "Yeah, but it's not a big deal," she said. "You guys have been talking about Cropsy a lot, and the big 'cliquey' talk and stuff." She smiled warily. "I guess I should have been more prepared for that. I just expected to get to camp and feel right at home right away, never realizing that there might be things I had missed."

Brynn nodded sympathetically. "It still wasn't cool of us. I've been spending so much time in rehearsals lately, I didn't even notice. I'm sorry."

Grace just squeezed her arm. "Forget it. You're going to be awesome in that show, and I'll be in the front row, cheering for you."

Brynn grinned. "Thanks."

\* \* \*

A throbbing dance beat was playing in the gym when Grace and Brynn joined their friends on the dance floor. Grace grabbed a hairclip from her pocket and piled all of her hair on top of her head, immediately moving to the music. All around them, groups and couples were dancing. Far on the perimeter, Grace spotted a familiar bespectacled face, laughing with one of his bunkmates and a couple of fourth-division girls. Her heart felt like it stopped for a minute. *He's flirting,* she thought. *I'm gone for a couple of hours, and he flirts with someone else. Priya was right.*

But as Grace watched him, he caught her eye and smiled. *Come over,* he gestured. Grace was torn. She took a deep breath and turned to Priya, who shrugged and gave her the thumbs up.

"I'll be right back," Grace promised.

Priya just smiled knowingly. "No hurry."

Spence pulled away from the rest of the group, moving over to stand by the concessions table as Grace approached him. He held out a cup of punch as Grace walked up.

"For the wandering adventurer," he said with a smile, "whose amazing tracking skills brought back a duplicitous reality-show wannabe."

Grace smiled, taking a sip of the punch. "Duplicitous?"

Spence nodded. "Big word, right? Get used to it, babe. Us journalism types have hot vocabularies."

Grace tried to hide her giggle with another sip.

"So," Spence went on. "Wanna dance?"

Grace looked up at him and put down her punch cup. Over his shoulder, she noticed one of the fourth-division girls he'd been talking to staring their way, looking surprised and upset. She probably felt exactly like Grace had felt when she'd spotted Spence talking to *her*. Grace had a sudden memory of the way Spence had seemed to light up when Chelsea, Gaby and Priya were flirting with him after newspaper. Grace felt like it really was genuine – Spence liked her. But it seemed like he liked a lot of people. In fact, it seemed as if he liked whoever was standing in front of him.

And then she remembered something: she thought she liked Spence, but she hadn't really thought about him at all while they'd been looking for Gaby.

Was she doing the same thing he was?

"Spence?" she said. "Can I tell you something?"

Spence nodded, picked up a punch cup of his own, and took a long sip. "Ahhh," he said. "Of course you can, Grace. You can tell me anything."

*I can*, she thought. It was really nice, actually. But that didn't necessarily mean they were soulmates.

"I like you," she said, and Spence grinned. "I love

being around you, because you're so easy to talk to and you make me laugh. But I think..." She paused. "I think I really like you as a friend."

Spence nodded slowly. Like always, he didn't seem surprised, angry, or defensive. He took a minute to absorb what she had to say, then smiled. "Okay. That's cool."

"I'm sorry," Grace said. "I hope I didn't mislead you."

"No biggie." Spence shrugged. "I think you're a cool chick, Grace. And you're a great partner on the arts beat. If you want to be just friends, that means I can still hang around you, so it's cool with me."

Grace smiled and looked back at the fourth-division girl, who was still watching. "I don't think you'll be lonely for long."

Spence just laughed. "Whatever. Neither will you." He leaned over and gave her a quick kiss on the cheek. "Have fun tonight. I'll see you tomorrow."

"See you tomorrow," Grace echoed. And Spence walked away, pausing once to turn around and give her a little wave before walking back to the younger girls.

Grace waved back and then walked over to Chelsea, who had been watching the scene. Priya, Jenna, Brynn and Jordan were all dancing nearby in a group.

"What *happened*?" Chelsea asked.

Grace shrugged. "No biggie. I told Spence I want to be just friends."

Chelsea's eyes bugged out. *"What?* Are you *kidding*?"

Grace shook her head and started dancing.

Chelsea's mouth dropped open. She leaned over to Priya and whispered in her ear.

*"What?"* Priya seemed to jump out of her skin as she turned to Grace. "You don't like *Spence*?"

Grace shook her head, still moving to the beat. "Not like that," she replied.

Priya and Chelsea looked at each other.

"We'd better comfort him," they both blurted at the same time. Before Grace could react, they were already halfway across the room, headed towards Spence.

Gaby caught Grace's eye as she turned around to watch Priya and Chelsea take off. "Oh, yeah," she said. *"That's* going to end well."

Grace just laughed and shrugged. "You know what? Not my problem any more."

Gaby smiled. The music changed right then, and Gaby jumped a little, recognizing the opening chords. "I *love* this song!"

"Me too," agreed Grace.

"Me three!" Brynn said.

"Me four!" said Jordan.

"Me five!" cried Jenna.

They all piled together, laughing and singing and trying to outdo one another with crazy dances. Grace couldn't get the silly smile off her face as she and Gaby screamed the chorus.

*I might have felt left out before,* she thought, *but I'm definitely back now.*

LEABHARLANN CHONTAE
Longfoirt

Turn the page for a sneak
preview of more

# SUMMER CAMP
# SECRETS

# THE CLIQUE

## CHAPTER ONE

"Yes!"

Tori awoke with a start and tried to prise her eyes open. It couldn't be morning already, could it? Her eyelids were so heavy they felt like rocks, but she managed to blink a few times and look around. A soft, grey light trickled through the cabin windows – definitely not bright enough for morning reveille. But then what had woken her up?

There was a giggle and someone dropped something on the floor across the bunk. Oh, great. Was someone pulling a prank in the middle of the night? Tori *so* didn't want to get involved. Pranks were so childish and pointless. Not to mention potentially damaging to personal property. She rolled over onto her side and lifted her pillow over her head to block out the noise. All she could do was hope it wasn't a silly string or toilet paper attack – something that would get the whole cabin up and screaming. Maybe if she ignored the pranksters, they would just leave her out of it.

"Red team rules!"

Suddenly someone jumped on Tori's bed and flipped her right onto her back. Tori whipped her pillow away to find Jenna Bloom hovering over her with a wild look in her eyes. Her curly brown hair stuck out in all directions, and she wore a brand-new red T-shirt over her pyjama bottoms. Behind her, the rest of the bunk started to rouse and yawn and look around to see what the commotion was. Even though it was pretty dark in the bunk, Tori could see that everyone else was just as confused as she was.

"Are you possessed?" Tori asked.

"Red team is going to kick Blue butt!" Jenna cheered. "And this year I'm not getting injured, so there's gonna be no stopping me! Woo-hoo!"

*Oh, God. Colour War!* Tori thought, her brain finally waking up enough to figure out what was going on. Jenna shook Tori a few times, chanting, "Red! Red! Red!" Then she climbed the bunk ladder to taunt Alex Kim.

"How do you know you're on Red?" Alex asked, fully alert as she climbed out of bed.

"T-shirts in our cubbyholes, baby! Colour War's early this year! Red all the way! Woo-hoo!"

Jenna was now in the centre of the cabin doing a sort of jerky, bizarro dance, like she was trying to bring on the rain or something. Tori rolled her eyes at Natalie Goode, who was just stretching her arms over her head in her own bed. Natalie shook her head in reply, clearly amused. Everyone knew Jenna lived for Colour War. The previous summer she had been all but shut out of participating because she had hurt her leg right before the yearly ritual began. Tori remembered feeling badly for Jenna, but also a little bit jealous of her. Tori would love to be excused from Colour War. The competition wasn't exactly Tori's cup of decaf chai tea. She had never been much of an athlete. Not like some of the other girls in her bunk. Tori was more into fashion and make-up and celebrity gossip than sports.

"I'm on Blue!" Alex announced, finding a new T-shirt in her cubby and yanking it on. Her dark hair staticked out and she smoothed it with one hand.

"I'm on Red!" Valerie exclaimed, high-fiving with Jenna. The beads at the ends of her multiple braids clicked as she lifted her hair out from the neck of her tee.

As the rest of the girls yanked out their T-shirts, Tori reluctantly crawled out of bed. She was aching to go back to sleep, but she didn't want to be labelled as a party pooper. Halfway across the room, Natalie tossed

Tori a blue T-shirt. It had that crisp, brand-new cotton smell. It said CAMP LAKEVIEW in small letters above the pocket, and COLOUR WAR in huge letters on the back.

"We're both on Blue!" Natalie announced, pulling her own shirt on over her head.

"Sweet," Tori replied. At least with Nat on her team she'd have someone like herself to bond with. And maybe laugh with over the silliness of the whole thing.

"Yeah, Blue team!" Grace called out, her red hair tucked into the collar of her new shirt. She slapped Tori's hand so hard it stung. "Blue team rules! Blue team rules! Blue team rules!"

Gaby, who was also wearing blue, joined Grace's chant. Candace stuck her arms through the holes of her own blue T-shirt and came over to stand quietly near Natalie and Tori. Candace was normally shy and usually either stayed quiet or repeated everything the other girls said. She had never been the chanting type.

"*Red* team rules! *Red* team rules! *Red* team rules!" Jenna shouted over Grace and Gaby. Priya, Valerie, Brynn and Chelsea all joined in with her. Soon Alex came in on the Blue side, and finally Natalie joined in as well, clearly not wanting to be outshined by Red. Tori simply smiled and leaned back against Grace's bunk bed behind her. She just did not have that competitive streak. Apparently Alyssa, who was on the Red team, didn't have one, either. She had put on her red shirt and crawled right back into bed.

"Red team rules!"

"*Blue* team rules!"

"Red team!"

"Blue team!"

"Red!"

"Blue!"

"Girls!"

All the lights in the cabin flicked on and everyone instantly fell silent. Tori turned around to find Belle, the counsellor for bunk 5A, standing in the doorway between her room and the main room, her short dark hair sticking straight up at the back. She wore her usual black tank top and grey shorts, and had a bit of black mascara smudged under her eyes. Not a good look for her.

"Okay, it is *way* too early for this. Would you kindly quiet down and go back to bed?" Belle said through her teeth. "I stayed up late waiting for you all to fall asleep so I could put your T-shirts in your cubbies, and I'm tired. And tiredness makes me *really* grumpy!"

"We noticed," Chelsea said under her breath, earning a round of laughter from the other girls.

"Now I want perfect silence until reveille, which

isn't for another...hour and a half," Belle said, checking her digital watch. "Is that understood?"

Belle was definitely a no-nonsense type of counsellor.

"Yes," everyone grumbled.

"Good."

Belle turned around and seconds later her cot squeaked under her weight. Everyone, including Tori, giggled through the tension as they returned to their beds. Tori climbed under the covers, but after a few minutes, whoops and hollers could be heard from other bunks all over the camp. Everyone was waking up early and finding their T-shirts. Even in her anti-Colour-War state of mind, a shiver of anticipation shot through Tori.

"I love Colour War so much," Jenna said dreamily.

Everyone laughed. So much for perfect silence.


The sun was up and shining, and all of bunk 5A were already gathered in a circle in the centre of the cabin later that same morning – red shirts on one side, blue on the other – when Natalie finally found the bottle of nail polish she was looking for and joined them. She plopped down between Grace and Alex, and placed her foam toe separators on each foot.

"What're you doing?" Gaby asked her. "Are you ever *not* primping?"

"It's for team spirit!" Natalie replied.

She produced the bottle of blue glitter polish from behind her back and quickly went to work on her toes.

"Wow! Nice touch!" Grace said. "But how'd you know you'd be on Blue?"

"I didn't. I have red, too," Natalie said. "But personally, I like blue *so* much better," she said pointedly, grinning at the Red side of the circle. "It's so much more original."

"Ugh! Natalie, could you get rid of that stuff? It's stinking up the place!" Jenna said, waving a hand in front of her face.

"It never bothered you before," Natalie said.

"It's not the nail polish. It's the *colour* that stinks!" Jenna replied.

The whole Red team cracked up and Natalie went back to her pedicure. "Ha ha. Hope for your sake they don't have a stand-up competition this year."

"Ooooh!" the Blue team chorused. Grace and Alex high-fived over Natalie's head. Natalie smirked. After three summers here, she was starting to get good at this trash-talking thing.

"Okay, ladies, let's call this little meeting to order!"

Belle announced, stepping out of her room with her clipboard. She was wearing a red T-shirt. The bunk's CIT, Clarissa, wore a blue shirt and stood next to Belle with two cloth bags in her hands — one red and the other blue. This was new. Natalie was officially curious, and she could tell by the looks on her friends' faces that they were as well.

"First, thank you for going back to sleep earlier this morning...even if it did take you another half-hour to quiet down," Belle said, earning a few giggles from the bunk. "Now that you all know which teams you're on, I have some Colour War related announcements."

"Colour War! Yeah!" Jenna cheered.

"I appreciate the enthusiasm, Jenna, but if you keep doing that I might never get through this," Belle said with a laugh.

"Sorry," Jenna said, pressing her lips together.

"Okay, since there are so few fifth-division campers this year, you guys will be combining with the sixth-division girls for some of the events," Belle said. "Only those which require large teams like soccer and capture the flag. For the rest of the events, you'll be strictly fifth division."

A murmur of interest ran through the circle. The sixth-division girls? They were so cool. And so... intimidating.

"Dr. Steve has also decided that this year, each team in each division will have a captain."

"Cool! I'm in!" Jenna announced, raising her hand.

"I'll do it!" Alex chimed in as well.

"Wait a second. What if I want to do it?" Gaby said.

Belle held up her hand. "In order to avoid having this turn into a popularity contest, I've decided to choose captains based on chance. The last thing this bunk needs is more rivalry."

Natalie nodded her head in agreement as she moved to her pinky toe. Since the very first day of camp this year, she and her bunkmates had been feuding about one thing or another, and only recently had everyone sort of calmed down and started to get along. If they voted for captains now, everyone would get upset all over again.

"So, in each of these bags there are six paper circles, five black and one gold," Belle said. Clarissa stepped forward and placed the red bag in front of Jenna and the blue bag in front of Candace. "Whoever picks the gold circle from each bag will be your captain."

"Go ahead! Pick!" Clarissa instructed.

Candace took a deep breath and reached into the blue bag. She came out with a black circle and sighed, clearly relieved. She handed the blue bag to Alex. Alex closed her eyes and yanked out...a black circle as well. She shrugged and gave the bag to Natalie. Nat quickly capped her nail polish, reached into the bag, and mixed up the circles inside. Then she grabbed one and pulled it out. Another black circle. She handed the bag to Grace.

"Come on, gold! Come on, gold!" Grace said. She reached in and yanked out...a black circle.

"Well, it's one of you two," Natalie said to Gaby and Tori. Secretly she was hoping Tori would get the gold. Gaby was bossy enough as it was. If she got to be captain, her head might swell to the point of explosion.

Tori reached into the bag and pulled out...the gold circle!

"Nice!" Natalie cheered.

"Captain Tori!" Grace cried out.

"Uh...great," Tori said, forcing a smile.


To find out what happens next read

# THE CLIQUE

Out now!

LONGFORD LIBRARY

3 0015 00323029 1

L192.8461

**LEABHARLÀNN CHONTAE LONGFOIRT**
**Longford County Library & Arts Services**

YA

This book should be returned on or before the latest
date shown below. Fines on overdue books will
accrue on a weekly basis or part thereof.

RP23342